The Golden Door

The Golden Door

EMILY RODDA

 Scholastic Press • *New York*

Library of Congress Cataloging-in-Publication Data

Rodda, Emily.
The golden door / Emily Rodda. — 1st ed.
p. cm.
Originally published: Parkside, S. Aust.: Omnibus Books, c2011.
Summary: At night the skimmers fly over the Wall looking for human prey and the people of Weld huddle in their houses, but after his two brothers set out through the magic doors in an attempt to find the Enemy and don't come back, young Rye knows that he must follow and find them.
ISBN 978-0-545-42990-0
1. Brothers — Juvenile fiction. 2. Monsters — Juvenile fiction. 3. Magic — Juvenile fiction. 4. Adventure stories. [1. Brothers — Fiction. 2. Monsters — Fiction. 3. Magic — Fiction. 4. Adventure and adventurers — Fiction.] I. Title.
PZ7.R5996Gol 2012
823.914 — dc23
2012014947

10 9 8 7 6 5 4 3 2 1   12 13 14 15 16

Printed in the U.S.A.   23

First American edition, October 2012

The text was set in Palatino.
Book design by Elizabeth B. Parisi

CONTENTS

1. The Brothers   1
2. The Challenge   11
3. The Parting   22
4. Nightmares   34
5. Fate   46
6. The Keep   54
7. The Chamber of the Doors   65
8. The Fell Zone   76
9. Downstream   88
10. The Fellan   97
11. Under the Stars   108
12. Nine Powers   118
13. The Kindness of Strangers   127
14. The Road to Oltan   137
15. Fleet   147
16. The Gifters   157
17. The Capture   168
18. City of Nightmare   177
19. The Flying Fish   188
20. The Fortress   200
21. The Chieftain   210
22. Midsummer Eve   219
23. Dark Waters   227
24. The Rock   238
25. Now or Never   246
26. Sunset   257

THE BROTHERS

I t was the season for skimmers, and this year more skimmers than ever were coming over the Wall of Weld.

From dusk till dawn, the beasts flapped down through the cloud that shrouded the top of the Wall. They showered on the dark city like giant, pale falling leaves, leathery wings rasping, white eyes gleaming, needle teeth glinting in the dark.

The skimmers came for food. They came to feast on the warm-blooded creatures, animal and human, that lived within the Wall of Weld.

On the orders of the Warden, the usual safety notices had been put up all over the city. Few people bothered to read them, because they were always the same. But this year, in Southwall, where Lisbeth the beekeeper lived with her three sons, they had been covered with disrespectful scrawls.

ATTENTION, CITIZENS OF WELD!
SKIMMER SAFETY

• Stay in your homes between dusk and dawn. *so the Skimmers know where to find you*

• Seal your windows, doors, and chimneys. *because Skimmers like a challenge!*

• Note that skimmers are almost blind, but are attracted by signs of life such as movement, light, heat, smell, and sound. *so stop breathing!*

• As is my duty, I cast the traditional spells of protection over Weld each day, but please remember—*though I know I have less magic in me than a Weld goat* your safety by night is your responsibility! *Not mine — I am tucked up safe in the Keep, HA HA!*

USELESS
The Warden of Weld

No one knew who was writing on the notices — or so the people of Southwall claimed when the Keep soldiers questioned them. Like everyone else in Weld, the Southwall citizens were very law-abiding. Most would never have dreamed of damaging one of the Warden's notices themselves. But many secretly agreed with the person who had done so.

2

Rye, the youngest of Lisbeth's sons, had the half-thrilled, half-fearful suspicion that his eldest brother, Dirk, might be responsible.

Dirk worked on the Wall as his father had done, repairing and thickening Weld's ancient defense against the barbarians on the coast of the island of Dorne. Brave, strong, and usually good-natured, Dirk had become increasingly angry about the Warden's failure to protect Weld from the skimmer attacks.

Sholto, the middle brother, thin, cautious, and clever, said little, but Rye knew he agreed with Dirk. Sholto worked for Tallus, the Southwall healer, learning how to mend broken bones and mix potions. The soldiers had questioned him when they had come to the healer's house seeking information. Rye had overheard him telling Dirk about it.

"Do not worry," Sholto had drawled when Dirk asked him anxiously what he had said in answer to the questions. "If I cannot bamboozle those fancily dressed oafs, I am not the man you think I am."

And Dirk had clapped him on the shoulder and shouted with laughter.

Rye hoped fervently that the soldiers would not question him, and to his relief, so far they had not. Rye was still at school, and no doubt the soldiers thought he was too young to know anything of importance.

As the clouded sky dimmed above them, and the Wall darkened around their city, the people of Weld closed their shutters and barred their doors.

Those who still followed the old magic ways sprinkled salt on their doorsteps and window ledges and chanted the protective spells of their ancestors. Those who no longer believed in such things merely stuffed rags and straw into the chinks in their mud-brick walls, and hoped for the best.

Lisbeth's family did all these things, and more.

Lisbeth sprinkled the salt and murmured the magic words. Dirk, tall and fair, followed her around the house, fastening all the locks. Dark, lean Sholto trailed them like a shadow, pressing rags soaked in the skimmer repellent he had invented into the gaps between the shutters and the crack beneath the door.

And Rye, red-haired and eager, watched them all as he did his own humble duty, clearing the table of Sholto's books and setting out the cold, plain food that was always eaten at night in skimmer season.

Later, in dimness, the three brothers and their mother huddled around the table, talking in whispers, listening to the hateful, dry rustling of the skimmers' wings outside.

"Folk at the market were saying that there was a riot in Northwall this morning," Lisbeth murmured. "They said that the Warden's signs were set on fire, and the crowd fought with the soldiers who tried to stop the damage. Can this be true? Citizens of *Weld* acting like barbarians?"

"It is true enough," Sholto said, pressing a hard-boiled duck egg against his plate to crack the pale blue shell as noiselessly as he could. "Skimmers killed three families in Northwall last night. It is only the first riot of many, I fear. When people are afraid, they do not think before they act."

Dirk snorted. "They are sick of the Warden's excuses. And they are right. Everyone on the Wall was talking of it today."

"And you most of all, Dirk, I imagine," said Sholto drily.

Dirk's eyes flashed. "Why not? It is obvious to everyone that a new leader must have risen among the barbarians — a warlord determined to conquer Weld at last. Every year, more skimmers come. Every year, we lose more food and more lives, and work on the Wall falls further behind. The Enemy is weakening us, little by little."

"We do not know there *is* an Enemy, Dirk," Sholto muttered. "For all we know, the skimmers come here of their own accord. For skimmers, Weld may be nothing but a giant feeding bowl, in which tender prey are conveniently trapped."

Rye's stomach turned over.

"Sholto!" Lisbeth scolded. "Do not say such things! Especially in front of Rye!"

"Why not in front of me?" Rye demanded stoutly, though the bread in his mouth seemed to have turned to dust. "I am not a baby!"

Sholto shrugged, carefully picking the last scrap of shell from his egg.

"We might as well face the truth," he said calmly. "A wall that cannot be climbed, and which has no gates, is all very well when it keeps dangers out. But it works two ways. It also makes prisoners of those who are inside it."

He bit into the egg and chewed somberly.

"The skimmers are being deliberately bred and sent!" Dirk insisted. "If they were natural to Dorne, they would have been flying over the Wall from the beginning. But the attacks began only five years ago!"

Sholto merely raised one eyebrow and took another bite.

Dirk shook his head in frustration. "Ah, what does it matter anyway?" he said, pushing his plate away as if he had suddenly lost his appetite. "What does it matter *why* the skimmers invade? They *do* invade — that is the important thing! Weld is under attack. And the Warden does nothing!"

"His soldiers fill the skimmer poison traps," Lisbeth murmured, anxious to restore peace at the table. "He has said that orphaned children can be cared for at the Keep. And he has at last agreed that the end-of-work bell should be rung an hour earlier, so people can arrive home well before —"

"*At last!*" Dirk broke in impatiently. "That is the point, Mother! The Warden has taken *years* to do things that a good leader would have done at once! If the Warden had not delayed cutting the hours of work, Father would not have been on the Wall at sunset in

6

the third skimmer season. He would still be with us now!"

"Don't, Dirk!" whispered Rye, seeing his mother bowing her head and biting her lip.

"I have to speak of it, Rye," said Dirk, his voice rising. "Our father was just one of hundreds of Wall workers who fell prey to skimmers because of the Warden's dithering!"

"Hush!" Sholto warned, raising his eyes to the ceiling to remind his brother of the skimmers flying above. And Dirk fell silent, pressing his lips together and clenching his fists.

✳

Like all the other citizens of Weld in skimmer season, Lisbeth and her sons went to bed early. What else was there to do, when sound was dangerous and the smallest chink of light might lead to a skimmer attack?

Rye lay in the room he shared with his brothers, listening to the rush of wings outside the shutters, the occasional scrabbling of claws on the roof.

He prayed that the wings would pass them by. He prayed that he, his mother, and his brothers would not wake, like those ill-fated families in Northwall, to find skimmers filling the house, and death only moments away.

He crossed his fingers, then crossed his wrists, in the age-old Weld gesture that was supposed to ward off evil. He closed his eyes and tried to relax, but he knew that sleep would not come easily. The closely shuttered room was stuffy and far too warm. Sholto's words at the dinner table kept echoing in his mind.

Weld may be nothing but a giant feeding bowl, in which tender prey are conveniently trapped. . . .

From Rye's earliest years, he had been told that inside the Wall of Weld there was safety, as long as the laws laid down by the Warden were obeyed.

Certainly, the laws were many. Sometimes even Rye had complained that they were *too* many.

He had nodded vigorously when Sholto had sneered that the citizens of Weld were treated like children too young to decide for themselves what was dangerous and what was not.

He had laughed when Dirk had made fun of the Warden's latest notices: *Citizens of Weld! Dress warmly in winter to avoid colds and chills. Children of Weld! Play wisely! Rough games lead to broken bones. . . .*

But at least he had felt safe — safe within the Wall.

Lying very still, his wrists crossed rigidly on his chest, Rye thought about that. He thought about Weld, and its Wall. Thought about the history he had learned and taken for granted. Thought, for the first time, about what that history meant.

Weld had existed for almost a thousand years, ever since its founder, the great sorcerer Dann, had fled with his followers from the savage barbarians and monstrous creatures that infested the coast of Dorne.

Turning his back on the sea, Dann had taken his

people to a place where the barbarians dared not follow. He had led them through the dangerous, forbidden ring of land called the Fell Zone, to the secret center of the island. And there, within a towering Wall, he had created a place of peace, safety, and magic — the city of Weld.

After Dann's time, the magic had slowly faded, but his Wall had remained. More than half of the city's workers labored on it every day, repairing and strengthening it. Every rock and stone in Weld, except for the stones that formed the Warden's Keep, had vanished into the Wall's vast bulk centuries ago. The workers used bricks of mud and straw to mend and thicken it now.

And as the Wall had thickened, little by little, it had crept ever closer to the great trench at its base — the trench from which the clay for bricks was dug.

The trench now circled Weld in the Wall's shadow like a deep, ugly scar. In the past, houses had been pulled down to make way for it. Soon, everyone knew, more would have to go.

The people did not complain. They knew that the Wall, and the Fell Zone beyond it, kept Weld safe. They had thought it always would.

Then the first skimmers had come. And now, after five years of invasions, it was clear to everyone that the days of safety were over.

The barbarians had at last found a way to attack Weld. Not by tunneling through the base of the Wall, as had always been feared, but by breeding creatures that could do what had once seemed impossible — brave the Wall's great height and fly over it.

And we are trapped inside, Rye thought.

Tender prey . . .

"This room is stifling!" he heard Dirk mutter to Sholto in the darkness. "I cannot breathe! Sholto, this cannot go on! The Warden must act!"

"Perhaps he will," Sholto whispered back. "The riot in Northwall must have shaken him. Tomorrow may bring some surprises."

THE CHALLENGE

The following day was the day of rest in Weld, but Dirk was up and dressed before the waking bell. He told Lisbeth that he was going to the square to hear the latest news, but Rye was sure that his brother planned to meet his friends to discuss the Northwall riot. Perhaps they were hoping that the people of Southwall could also be roused to protest.

Sholto must have thought as Rye did, because as Dirk was leaving, he casually said that he would walk with him.

"I will come, too," Rye said instantly.

He could see that Dirk and Sholto did not want his company, but he knew that they could not refuse to take him with them without raising Lisbeth's suspicions.

The brothers left through the back garden, where the bees were already humming around the honey hedge, and the bell tree, heavy with ripening fruit, basked in the early morning sun.

Keeping well to the right, as Weld citizens always did, they began walking briskly through the maze of short, straight streets that led to the square.

Every street was just wide enough to allow two goat carts to pass one another. Every street was closely lined with identical houses — small, mud-brick houses like Lisbeth's house, and every other house in Weld.

At this early hour, most people were still busily unsealing their doors and windows, and checking the crops in their tiny back gardens for skimmer damage. Most looked tired and strained after a night of little sleep, but as was the Weld way, they looked up from their work and exchanged friendly greetings with the young men as they passed by.

They all knew and admired Dirk. They all knew that Sholto would one day be the Southwall healer. And they all bought honey and bell fruit preserves from Lisbeth in the market.

Two of Dirk's friends, Joliffe and Crell, were just leaving Joliffe's home when the brothers reached it. It seemed they, too, were going to the square. By the way Joliffe and Crell glanced disapprovingly at him, Rye could tell he had been right about a planned meeting.

He hung back a little, and after a while, as he had hoped, the other four half-forgot he was there, and began to talk freely. Sure enough, the talk was all about the Northwall riot.

"The Northwall people were quite right," Joliffe muttered as they passed a skimmer poison trap and skirted the few dead skimmers lying in their path. "The Warden is a pompous fool. Why should we put up with him?"

"His family has governed Weld since ancient times," Crell said anxiously. "Ever since —"

"Ever since the Sorcerer Dann died, leaving Weld's care to his friend, the first Warden of Weld . . ." Dirk chanted in a mocking, singsong voice.

". . . who was great in magic, and so on and so on," Joliffe finished for him impatiently. "We all know the story, Crell, you ninny! We have heard it a thousand times. But what of it?"

"What of it indeed?" Dirk snorted. "The first Warden was only appointed caretaker of Weld, Crell — *caretaker*, not king. There was no reason at all for the title to be passed on from father to son as it has been. If a drop of magic blood runs in the present Warden's veins, I am a — a —"

"A Weld goat?" Joliffe suggested, raising his eyebrows, and Crell and Dirk laughed.

"The present Warden has no sons," Sholto put in quietly. "He only has a daughter."

He shrugged as his companions stared at him.

"People are strange and set in their ways," he said. "Of course there is no reason why the Warden should not be female. But once the father-to-son tradition has been broken, people may listen to us

13

when we call for change. If we bide our time, we may get what we want peacefully."

"I never thought of that!" Crell exclaimed. He, at least, plainly found the idea of a peaceful solution very appealing.

Rye felt a rush of admiration for Sholto. Sholto was not easy and affectionate, like Dirk. He was sometimes impatient — even cold. Rye often suspected he preferred books to people. But he could be trusted to think things through, coolly and carefully.

Dirk shook his head. "You may be right, Sholto, but it would take too long. Weld needs change *now* if it is to survive, and the Warden has plenty of life in him yet."

"Quite so," said Joliffe with the trace of a sneer. "Fine plans for the future might suit those with their heads in the clouds, but we who are practical must deal with the present."

Rye had noticed that Joliffe often made sly digs at Sholto. Perhaps, Rye thought, Joliffe was a little jealous of Dirk's loyalty to his clever brother.

"Shh!" Crell hissed. "Soldiers!"

Sure enough, three figures in the crisp white tunics and red leggings worn by the soldiers of the Keep had rounded a corner just ahead and were marching toward them in single file. The heavy gold braid on the soldiers' sleeves and shoulders glinted in the soft morning light. The white plumes on their helmets nodded and swayed.

Fancily dressed oafs . . . Sholto's contemptuous

words whispered in Rye's mind, and for the first time in his life, he stared at Keep soldiers without respectful admiration.

"What business could soldiers have had in the square so early in the day?" Dirk muttered.

"They must have been expecting trouble," said Joliffe, sounding gleeful.

Sholto shook his head. "If that were so, they would not have left so soon. And there would be more than three of them."

Joliffe shot him an annoyed glance but said nothing.

The soldiers passed by, nodding politely, as Keep soldiers were trained to do to show they were no threat to law-abiding citizens.

Dirk, Sholto, Joliffe, and Crell returned the greetings casually. Rye muttered and ducked his head. Something unusual had happened; he was sure of it. He could feel the soldiers' excitement — kept well under control but radiating from them like heat.

"Perhaps there was skimmer damage in the square overnight," Crell said. "Maybe there have been more deaths!"

Everyone but Sholto crossed fingers and wrists.

But when they reached the square, they found that the soldiers' errand had been something completely unexpected.

A large new notice had been fixed to the wall of the long, low meetinghouse that took up one side of the square. A small knot of people stood before the notice, chattering excitedly. Dirk, Joliffe, Crell, and Sholto ran to look, with Rye hurrying behind them.

ATTENTION MALES 18 YEARS AND OVER!

I hereby call for volunteers willing to leave Weld on a perilous quest to find and destroy the enemy responsible for the skimmer invasions.

Volunteers will leave the city by an ancient way that until now has been a secret of the Keep. They will be given supplies but must provide their own weapons. For secrecy, each volunteer must leave the city alone.

The hero who succeeds in destroying the Enemy and saving his people will receive the hand of my daughter in marriage and be named my heir as Warden of Weld.

If you are of age and wish to volunteer, please report to the Keep without delay.

The Warden of Weld

Rye gaped at the notice, his head reeling.

All his life he had believed that the Wall of

Weld was an unbroken circle, with no way in or out. He had never doubted it for a moment. It had been more than belief. It had been something he had *known*, as surely as he knew his own name. And now, suddenly . . .

"Ha!" Dirk breathed. "Sholto, do you see that? Do you see it?"

"I can read," Sholto murmured. "So . . . old Tallus's tale of the Sorcerer's secret way through the Wall is true after all. Who would have believed it?"

Rye looked up at him and felt a chill.

Sholto looked quite calm — even slightly bored — but no one who knew him as well as Rye did could miss the fact that his dark, clever eyes were glowing as if lit by a flame from within.

Rye knew that Sholto was thinking of what he could learn beyond the Wall. He was imagining himself tracking the skimmers to their source in the Fell Zone, where he was sure they bred, and finding a way to destroy them.

The glow in Sholto's eyes was the thirst for knowledge. And it was strong — strong enough to smother his natural caution.

Sholto is not yet eighteen, Rye told himself feverishly. *I do not have to worry about him. He is too young to accept the Warden's challenge.*

But then he looked past Sholto to Dirk, and fear gripped his heart. Dirk, a head taller than Sholto and broader in the shoulders by far, was almost twenty.

And Dirk was punching the air, his face alive with excitement.

"At last, Joliffe!" Dirk cried, clapping his friend on the back. "At last, a chance to do something to help ourselves! By the Wall, I cannot believe it!"

"Dirk, no!" Rye burst out. "You must not go!"

"Are you mad, Rye?" snapped Joliffe. "How can we turn our backs on an offer like this? Do you not see the prize for success? Did you not read the sign?"

"Did *you*?" Rye retorted angrily. "Did you not see that each volunteer must leave the city alone? How can one man defeat the Enemy who is sending the skimmers? It would take an army!"

Joliffe snorted. "Dirk, Crell, and I will join up outside the Wall, never fear."

"And as for an army, Rye," Dirk put in, "well, for once, the Warden is in the right. In a quest such as this, a small band, moving stealthily, is better than an army. It can find out the Enemy's secrets and weaknesses without raising the Enemy's fears."

His eyes were shining. "Even one man could do it, if he was brave and determined enough. Look what the Sorcerer Dann did in ancient times! He saved his followers from the barbarians single-handed."

"But that was then!" Rye burst out. "This is now! And the Sorcerer Dann had magic to aid him! Powerful magic! You have no magic, Dirk."

"None of us do," Crell said dismally. "Magic is dead in Weld, or so my grandmother says."

"Magic is dead in Weld because it never existed in the first place," Sholto drawled. "When will you people accept that the old tales are just that — old tales, that have no foundation in truth? Dann's so-called 'magic powers' were simply a mixture of quick wits and good sense, with a few ingenious inventions thrown in."

"Inventions like your famous skimmer repellent, no doubt." Joliffe smirked, nudging Crell in the ribs.

"No doubt," Sholto said, unruffled. "Ignorant people often call things magic when they do not understand them."

Joliffe decided to ignore him. He puffed out his chest and stretched out his arms to embrace Dirk and Crell.

"So, comrades! Tomorrow we go to the Keep to volunteer! Agreed?"

"Agreed!" Dirk and Crell both shouted, though it seemed to Rye that Crell looked uneasy.

"Excellent!" Joliffe declared, rubbing his hands. "Now, I see that the tavern has opened. Let us go and drink to our success!"

Dirk hesitated, glanced at his brothers, then shook his head. "It is a little early for me," he said.

Joliffe laughed. "Oh, of course," he jeered. "Sholto and Rye are too young to enter the tavern. But surely they can find their own way home?"

"It is a little early for me," Dirk repeated with a smile. And seeing that he would not be persuaded,

Joliffe shrugged and made for the tavern himself, with Crell trotting by his side.

"Dirk, you cannot go beyond the Wall," Rye whispered, the moment they were alone. "It is too dangerous! Think what Mother will say!"

Sholto looked disdainful. But Dirk ruffled his youngest brother's hair affectionately.

"Of course I must go, Rye," he said. "There is danger, yes, but nothing is more important than saving Weld — nothing! Besides, think what it will mean to us if I succeed!"

And think what it will mean to us if you never come back, Dirk, Rye could not help retorting in his mind, though he did not speak the words aloud, and felt disloyal even thinking them.

Surely, if anyone could find and destroy the Enemy of Weld, Dirk could. His strength and courage made him a natural leader. He had been made a Foreman after only two years on the Wall and, young as he was, he was respected by his men. How many times had Rye heard his mother say that their father would have been proud to see how closely his eldest son had followed in his footsteps?

"Our home and our people would be safe!" Dirk was rushing on. "And in time I would be Warden!"

"On condition that you marry the present Warden's daughter," Sholto reminded him drily. "Oh, our Warden may be a coward, terrified of new ideas, and slow to act. But he is cunning."

"What do you mean?" asked Rye. He was so troubled that he was finding it hard to think clearly.

Sholto laughed shortly. "Why, do you not see it? By offering his daughter's hand in marriage to the hero who becomes his heir, the Warden has ensured that *his* descendants will continue to rule Weld!"

"I admit that the Warden's daughter is the fly in the honey," Dirk said ruefully. "I have no wish to marry someone I have never seen. But perhaps it would not be so bad. Perhaps the Warden's daughter is kind, clever, and beautiful!"

"Perhaps she is spiteful, stupid, and ugly!" Sholto smirked. "What then?"

Dirk laughed. "Then I will say that I will become the heir but will not take the daughter! If I come home triumphant, the Warden will not dare to refuse me."

Again he ruffled Rye's hair, his broad, handsome face alive with hope.

"Imagine it, Rye! Imagine if I was Warden of Weld! Think of the good we could do! Think of the changes we could make! How often have we talked of it?"

Rye felt hot, treacherous tears burning behind his eyes. "But that was only . . . *talk*!" he cried. "I never thought it was *real*!"

Dirk's hand dropped from Rye's head onto his shoulder.

"Then you did not understand, Rye," he said soberly. "It was very real. Mother knows this. She will understand that I must go."

THE PARTING

And so it proved. The next morning, with his mother's blessing, Dirk marched away from Southwall, his father's skimmer hook over his shoulder and the cheers of his neighbors ringing in his ears. Joliffe, Crell, and a handful of other brave men went with him.

The volunteers were singing as they swung along the broad, straight road that led west to the Keep. Those they had left behind stood watching until they were out of sight.

"We should feel very proud," said Lisbeth, putting her arm around Rye's shoulders. "Dirk is doing what must be done, to save us all."

But watching the small band of marchers disappearing into the distance, Rye felt only terrible fear, and an aching sense of loss.

A few days later, Crell slunk back into Southwall with a rag tied around his leg. He said he had hurt his ankle at the Keep, so had been forced to come home. He was certainly limping, sometimes more and sometimes less, but he refused to see Tallus the healer. Few believed in his injury, though no one said so aloud.

Shamed and sullen, Crell said little in answer to the townspeople's eager questions. The Keep had been crowded with volunteers from every part of the city. The group from Northwall had been the largest and noisiest of all. Crell had lost sight of Dirk, Joliffe, and the others from Southwall. He had not been shown the secret way out of Weld.

He retreated to his home and stayed out of sight for days. His mother, who was Lisbeth's friend, clearly felt disgraced. But Rye could see, deep in her shadowed eyes, a flicker of relief.

The house seemed very empty without Dirk. His cheerful whistling no longer brightened the early mornings. Dinners around the table were dull without his whispered talk, teasing, and laughter. And at night, Rye lay listening to the sounds of the skimmers with only the silent Sholto for company. Dirk's empty, neatly made bed seemed to dominate the hot, still room.

Lisbeth and Sholto went on with their lives just as they had before Dirk left. Lisbeth tended her bees and sold the honey at her market stall. Sholto continued grinding powders and mixing potions for Tallus the healer, examining dead skimmers in Tallus's workroom, and studying his books in every spare moment.

Rye did not understand how they could. He missed Dirk so much! He dreamed of him every night, and every morning woke to the misery of his brother's absence. It was as if a great hole had been torn in his world, and it changed everything.

School lessons seemed pointless. Games seemed pointless. His friends talked constantly about the adventures Dirk, Joliffe, and the others must be having beyond the Wall. Their chatter seemed to rasp on Rye's nerves like sandpaper, and he began to spend more time alone.

"You must have courage, Rye," Lisbeth murmured to her youngest son when she found him moping in the shade of the bell tree one afternoon. "We all miss Dirk, my dear, but what must be, must be."

Rye looked up into her face and saw how pale she was. He saw the shadows beneath her eyes, and a line between her brows that he had never noticed before. With a pang, he at last understood that Lisbeth was suffering even more than he was, but was bearing her pain bravely, for all their sakes.

He nodded and forced a smile, suddenly feeling much older.

"There will be news of Dirk very soon, I am sure of it," his mother told him.

"I am sure of it, too," Rye replied as firmly as he could.

But the weeks slipped by, and no news came.

The fruit on the bell tree ripened. Rye picked the juicy yellow bells, Lisbeth preserved them, and the pantry filled with jars of golden sweetness.

Usually, Lisbeth kept some jars for the family's use, and took the rest to the market. This year, all the jars would have to be sold. Sholto earned very little from Tallus because he was still learning the healer's art, and now that Dirk's wages were no longer flowing in, the family needed every coin it could get.

The skimmers kept coming. More crops were lost, more beasts perished, and more people died.

Then, as the heat slowly became less, the attacks became fewer, and at last, stopped altogether. In Lisbeth's garden, the leaves of the bell tree colored and fell, and the bare, pruned branches were stubby and stark against the white of the beehives.

And still Dirk did not return. Nor did any of the other men who had marched, singing, away from Southwall. Lisbeth's eyes grew more shadowed. Sholto became more silent than ever.

The Warden's notice remained on the wall of the meetinghouse in the square like a memorial to those who had gone, growing more faded with every passing day.

At last, the air began to warm once more, and the sun shone strongly in the misty skies of Weld. The bell tree sprouted and became a glorious umbrella of yellow blossoms, humming with bees. Then the blossoms fell

25

to form a perfect golden circle on the ground and tiny green fruit began to form.

And as the fruit swelled and ripened, the skimmer invasions began again.

Just over a year after Dirk left, Rye and Sholto came home to find Lisbeth sitting in her chair by the fireplace, staring at the cold ashes in the grate.

Her hands were on her lap. In one, she held a gold brooch in the shape of a flower. The other clutched a small scroll. Tight-lipped, Sholto freed the scroll from her fingers. As he unrolled it, Rye pushed close so he, too, could read what was written upon it.

To *Lisbeth of Southwall,*

It is with great regret that I inform you that your son *Dirk* is now officially believed to have perished beyond the Wall. Please accept my profound sympathy.

I enclose a token which you may wear with pride. Weld will always be grateful for *Dirk's* brave sacrifice. If, as a result of *Dirk's* loss, you are in any difficulty, please report to the Keep for help without delay.

Yours in sorrow,

The Warden of Weld

"Our precious Warden must have sent out many of these today," Sholto muttered, looking down his nose at the scroll. "So many, indeed, that it would have taken too long for him to write each note individually. Most of this message was written for him. He has simply filled in the spaces and signed at the bottom!"

Lisbeth snatched the scroll back. With trembling fingers, she fastened the gold flower to the bodice of her plain brown dress.

"Dirk was a hero," she said, her voice shaking. "He died like his father, doing what he thought was right. If you wish to sneer, Sholto, please sneer where I cannot hear you!"

Sholto turned away, his face expressionless. He began walking to the back of the house, where his supplies of skimmer repellent were kept.

"We had better begin locking up," he said to Rye over his shoulder. "I will fetch the rags."

Rye knelt by his mother's chair and put his hand on her arm. A terrible ache was swelling in his throat and chest, but he made himself speak.

"Mother, Dirk may come back to us yet, whatever the Warden says," he whispered, trying to make himself believe it. "He has been away a long time, but there is no proof that — that he is lost."

Lisbeth covered his hand with one of hers. Her fingers were very cold. With the other hand, she fingered the delicate brooch pinned to her dress.

"And — and Sholto was not sneering at Dirk,

Mother," Rye rushed on. "He was just . . . trying to shut out the pain."

He had not planned what he was going to say, but as the words left his mouth, he knew that they were true.

"Yes," Lisbeth murmured through dry lips. "I should not have spoken to poor Sholto so. But . . . oh, Dirk, my tall, laughing Dirk! My firstborn! How can I bear it?"

She began to weep bitterly. Rye stayed crouched beside her for a while, but at last, he crept away to help Sholto seal the shutters. By the time they had finished, Lisbeth had gone to her room.

As the sun went down, Sholto and Rye ate in silence.

No one sprinkled the salt before we sealed the house, Rye thought. No one chanted the spells of protection.

But he said nothing aloud. He knew that Sholto would scoff at the idea that magic did anything that the skimmer repellent did not do a hundred times better.

That night, Rye lay awake for many hours. He thought that Sholto did, too, though there was no sound at all from Sholto's bed.

He was just drifting into an uneasy doze when he was jolted awake. Distant crashes and screams were mingling with the muffled beats of the skimmers' wings. He gasped and sat up, his heart pounding.

"Be still, Rye!" he heard Sholto hiss in the darkness. "They are not attacking us. But it is somewhere very near."

Rye sat rigidly, blinking in the dark, trying to resist the ghastly images of what must be happening just a few streets away.

After a few long minutes, the awful screams abruptly ceased. But the dry rasping of the skimmers' wings went on and on and on. . . .

❋

In the morning, when Rye and Sholto went out together to hear the news, they found the streets of Southwall seething with a tale of horror. The mother, father, sister, and grandmother of Dirk's friend Joliffe were all dead.

A back window of the family's home had been found yawning open, each of its shutters ferociously clawed and dangling from one twisted hinge. Five dead skimmers lay among the ravaged bones in the main bedroom, showing how valiantly Joliffe's parents had fought for their lives, and the lives of the others in the house.

The neighbors had heard it all and were numb with shock. They were also plainly filled with shame because they had not tried to save the doomed family, though no one blamed them for a moment. Everyone knew that to open one's doors when skimmers were overhead meant certain death.

The neighbors said that on the day of the tragedy Joliffe's parents had received a letter from the Warden.

The letter, enclosing a gold badge in the shape of a flower, had declared that Joliffe was now officially believed to be dead.

Joliffe's parents had never lost hope until that moment. Who could wonder that the family, distracted by grief, had failed to seal the shutters properly, so that the hunting skimmers found a gap through which to attack?

We would have suffered the same fate if it had not been for Sholto, Rye thought, glancing at his stony-faced brother. *It was Sholto who thought to seal our doors and windows last night. It was Sholto who put aside his grief to do what had to be done. It is because of him that he, Mother, and I are alive today.*

But he knew better than to try to thank or praise Sholto for what he had done.

Sholto was filled with rage. Rye could feel it. Not a muscle of Sholto's face moved, but Rye knew that his mind was burning with thoughts of Dirk, his lost brother; of Joliffe, though Joliffe had never liked him; of Joliffe's family, horribly dead.

"This must stop," Sholto muttered as he and Rye turned for home. "There must be a way."

Rye knew that he required no answer. He was speaking not to Rye, but to himself.

So Rye was grieved but not wholly surprised when, the next morning, he woke to find Sholto's bed empty and a letter for Lisbeth lying on the table in the living room.

My dear Mother,

I have gone to the Keep to volunteer for the Warden's quest. The notice is still on view, so I assume the offer is still open to all who are of age. As you will remember, I turned eighteen two weeks ago.

I am no hero, like my brother Dirk. I feel, however, that I must do what I can to find out the source of the skimmer invasions. I have explained my point of view to Tallus the healer, who agrees with me.

I fear my decision will grieve you, so I am going quietly, without fuss. I have taken one of the lanterns. I hope you will not mind this. I do not think you will miss my pay. It is so little that I doubt it covers the food I eat.

Please take care over the coming weeks. The skimmer attacks in Southwall are certain to increase, following the deaths of Joliffe's family. Once skimmers have tasted blood in a place, they remember and return there seeking more.

There are good supplies of repellent in the back room. Be sure Rye soaks the rags well each day, before use.

Sholto

Rye stared at the note — at one line in particular.

As you will remember, I turned eighteen two weeks ago.

Sholto had turned eighteen! But there had been no party, with all the neighbors invited in to feast and celebrate, as there had been for Dirk when he came of age. In the fear for Dirk's fate, and at the height of skimmer season, Sholto's eighteenth birthday had passed almost unnoticed.

Except by Sholto himself, Rye thought.

The note seemed so cold. It said nothing of love, or regret at parting. For a moment, Rye was tempted to tear it up and throw the scraps into the cooking fire.

But of course he could not do that. The note was for Lisbeth, and Lisbeth had to read it.

He heard a sound behind him, and turned. His mother was standing in the doorway of her room, a shawl thrown over her nightgown, a long braid hanging down her back. Her tired eyes searched Rye's face, then fell to the note in his hand.

"Sholto . . ." Rye managed to say.

He went to his mother and awkwardly held out the paper, but Lisbeth made no attempt to take it.

"He has gone, then," she said dully.

Stunned, Rye nodded.

"I knew it would be so," said Lisbeth. "But I had hoped it would not be so soon. Ah, Sholto . . ."

"They may not let him go, Mother," Rye burst out, desperate to comfort her. "Sholto can fight in his way, but he is not very strong. They may send him home again, like Crell."

To his surprise, the corners of Lisbeth's mouth curved in a wry half smile. "Sholto is not Crell," she said. "Sholto wants to go. And he will get what he wants, by trickery if he has to. It has always been the same, from the time he was a tiny child."

She sighed. Her eyes were far away. "So quiet, he was, my dark, determined little Sholto. But in his way, he was more of a handful than Dirk. At least I always knew where Dirk was. He made noise enough for two children and could not keep still for a moment. But Sholto . . ."

The smile faded, and for the first time, her lips trembled.

"Sholto will get what he wants," she repeated. "By fair means or foul, he will go beyond the Wall."

NIGHTMARES

It was strange, Rye thought, that the house seemed so silent without Sholto. Sholto had said so little. Yet somehow, now he had gone, the very walls seemed to echo, as if they missed his calm, watchful presence.

At night, Rye now dreamed of Sholto as well as Dirk. The faces of both his brothers loomed at him out of the darkness, first one and then the other. Sometimes their mouths moved, but he could not hear their voices because of a rhythmic, pounding sound that echoed through every dream like a gigantic drum.

The bell tree marked the changing of the seasons, and Sholto did not return. At school, Rye's friends no longer bothered to ask him to join their games. They knew he would refuse.

Rye spent his lunch hours reading. He had begun borrowing history books from the book room, hoping to learn something — anything — about the land outside the Wall, the land that had swallowed his brothers.

But he found very few facts that he did not already know. The story of Dann was like a fable, told always in the same way and with very little detail. It was as if all history had begun when Weld was made, and everything before that was darkness.

The only maps of Dorne that Rye could find were all exactly the same as the one that hung on the wall of the Southwall schoolroom, beside the Warden's portrait. Rye could probably have drawn this map by heart, having stared at it so often during boring lessons. But still he spent one lunch hour copying it carefully.

He carried the scrap of paper home with the sour feeling that he had been wasting his time. But the following morning, he woke early and looked again at the map he had drawn.

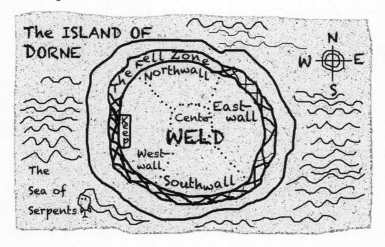

As Rye stared at the map, really *seeing* it for the first time, his heart sank. He understood why the Warden had been so sure that Dirk, Joliffe, and the other volunteers were no more.

None of the volunteers could have simply lost his way home. Weld dominated the island. Its wall had to be visible from every part of Dorne.

I must accept it, Rye thought fiercely. Dirk is dead. And by now, Sholto is probably dead, too.

But he could not accept it. And as he ran his finger over the map, tracing imaginary paths from the Keep of Weld to the sea, he felt a growing certainty that Dirk and Sholto were alive — alive somewhere beyond the Wall.

Rye knew that he would not be able to explain this feeling to anyone, even Lisbeth. There was no logic to it, no sense. But it persisted, burning in the center of his being like a small stubborn flame that would not go out.

Skimmer season arrived again, more terrifying than ever before. The beasts flew over Weld in such numbers that the walls and roofs of the dark, sealed houses seemed to vibrate with the sound of their passing. It was very hot, and there were wild tales of folk who had run mad in their stifling rooms, throwing open their windows and taking great gulps of night air before skimmers overwhelmed them.

As Sholto had predicted, attacks became more

frequent in Southwall, especially in the streets near Joliffe's home. Deaths were now so commonplace that they were barely noted except by those close to the people who had been lost.

The Warden's skimmer warning signs had gone up on every corner as usual, but no one touched them. The citizens of Southwall had lost the taste for protest, it seemed.

"And there have been no more riots, in Northwall or anywhere else," Lisbeth said one evening when the house had been sealed as tightly as a jar of bell fruit preserves, and she and Rye had sat down to eat. "That is something to be grateful for, at least."

Rye nodded absently. That afternoon, he had counted the buckets of skimmer repellent remaining in the storeroom. He thought there was enough repellent left to last until the end of the present season. But what of the next?

Sholto will be back before then, he told himself.

But a few days later, he came home from school to find Lisbeth wearing two gold flower badges instead of one. Lying on the table was the scroll bearing the Warden's seal and declaring that Sholto was officially regarded as lost.

"Do not believe it, Mother!" Rye cried fiercely. "Sholto is not dead! And neither is Dirk!"

Perhaps Lisbeth had wept when the Warden's letter first arrived, but she was tearless now. She shook her head and turned away.

"Stop hoping, Rye," she said. "We have our home, and we have each other. Let that be enough."

That night, Rye dreamed more vividly than ever.

He saw Dirk crawling through a dark, narrow space, his face blackened and running with sweat. He saw Sholto sitting in what appeared to be a cave, writing furiously in a notebook. He saw vast, scaled bodies beating water to foam. He saw monstrous feathered shadows flying through cloud. He saw the trunks of trees melting into the shapes of men and women with hair that flew around their heads like flames.

And rising above the rhythmic pounding sound that he had learned to expect, there were harsh cries and the deep, vibrating music of a vast bell or gong.

He woke, shaking, in the darkness and stayed awake till dawn. It was far better to lie listening to the skimmers than to risk dreaming again.

He left home at his usual time, but he did not go to school. Instead, obeying an impulse he could not really explain, he went to the house of Tallus the healer.

No patients were waiting. A scrappy note had been pinned to the door of the healer's office.

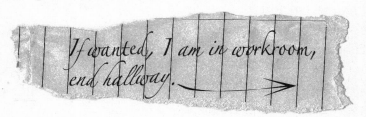

If wanted, I am in workroom, end hallway.

Rye ventured down the hallway and hesitated outside the workroom door.

He had not seen Tallus face-to-face since, as a small child, he had fallen from Dirk's back and dislocated his shoulder. He had never forgotten the experience.

"See this, young Rye?" Tallus had barked, pulling at the fluff of white hair that ringed his bald scalp. "Once it was as red as yours. Can you believe that?"

Openmouthed, Rye had shaken his head, for a moment quite forgetting the pain in his shoulder.

"Red hair means luck, they say," Tallus had said. "Luck — and other things."

For some reason, he had then glanced at Rye's mother, who had looked worried and shaken her head, very slightly.

"But white hairs," Tallus had gone on smoothly, "mean old age. And as you can see, I am very old indeed. If you can count the red hairs I have left on my head, you will know how many years I have to live. Will you do that for me? I should like to know."

And while Rye, fascinated, was trying to find even one red hair in that mass of white, the healer had made a quick movement, and suddenly the arm that had been twisted out of shape was straight again, and the pain had gone.

Remembering, Rye smiled, and knocked at the door.

"What is it?" a gruff voice shouted.

"It is Rye, Sholto's brother, Healer Tallus!" Rye called. "I need to speak to you . . . if you please."

"Oh, very well," the voice replied ungraciously. "Come in."

Rye opened the door. He saw a large room lined with shelves of labeled jars. Pots bubbled on the stove in one corner. The room was filled with steam and reeked of skimmers.

Tallus, a small, crabbed figure wrapped in a stained white apron and wearing thick eyeglasses, was standing at a bench vigorously sharpening a thin-bladed knife.

"Shut that door!" he yelled, swinging around and brandishing the knife. "Do you want to stink the whole house out?"

Rye made haste to do as he was told, took two steps through the billowing steam, and stopped dead.

A dead skimmer, the largest he had ever seen, lay on a long table in the center of the room. Foam clotted its snarling jaws and ratlike snout. Its eyes were open, glazed in death so they looked like chips of white china. Its body, covered in pale, velvety fuzz, was as big as the body of a half-grown goat. Its leathery wings, spread wide and pinned flat, covered the table from end to end.

"Yes, they are larger this year," Tallus said, seeing his visitor's eyes widen. "And this one is still quite young, by the looks of the wings, which tend to become ragged with age. See how strong the spurs have become, too!"

He limped to the table and with the point of the knife he lifted one of the spines that jutted from the monster's legs, just above the razor-sharp claws. The spur was half as long as the knife blade and twice as broad.

"The eyes," Rye murmured, gazing in fascination at the skimmer's blind white stare. "I have never seen them open before. I did not realize they were so —"

"Yes, this is a perfect specimen!" said Tallus, looking down at the skimmer with satisfaction. "Almost undamaged and very fresh. I found it only this morning in the water trap your brother made for me. A clever piece of work, that trap. You simply float spoiled goat meat in a tank of water, and —"

"Sholto has been declared lost," Rye blurted out, and to his horror, he felt sudden tears burning behind his eyes and heard his voice quaver.

"Indeed?" Tallus murmured absently, moving the knifepoint to a swelling beside the skimmer's spur and probing gently. "Has he been away a year already? Bless me, where has the time gone?"

Rye bit back a furious retort. What sort of master was Tallus, to encourage Sholto to go into danger and then care so little about what happened to him?

He took a deep breath to calm himself and was relieved to find that his anger had driven away the threatened tears. The blood rushed into his face as he realized that perhaps this was exactly what Tallus had intended.

"There, you see that?" Tallus said, adjusting his eyeglasses and nodding down at the skimmer.

Rye looked and saw the dribble of pale green fluid oozing from the swelling beneath the knifepoint.

"These spur venom pouches are at least twice the size of those I have seen on other young skimmers," said Tallus. "That proves what I have been saying for years. As a species, skimmers adapt very quickly to conditions."

"What . . . conditions?" Rye asked weakly.

"Why, a reliable source of nourishing prey!" Tallus exclaimed. "Prey that fights back, but which can be paralyzed almost instantly by skimmer venom."

"By 'nourishing prey' you mean us, I suppose," said Rye, feeling sick.

"Certainly!" cried Tallus. "Venom has become an important weapon for skimmers who prey on us. So, if my theory is correct, more and more young with large venom pouches will be born over the next few years."

He straightened and wiped his knife blade on his apron.

"Sholto and I think that whatever creatures the skimmers fed on before they discovered us were slower and more defenseless than we are, so rarely had to be paralyzed before being consumed," he went on enthusiastically. "Sholto goes so far as to suggest that the previous prey might have been a species of turtle because of the powerful grinding back teeth we observed in all the early skimmer specimens. Such teeth would be ideal for reducing hard shell to powder, you know."

Rye nodded again, feeling sicker than ever.

"Well, we shall soon know the truth of it," Tallus said confidently. "Sholto will certainly have settled the question by the time he returns."

Rye's heart gave a great thud.

"Healer Tallus!" he gasped. "You believe that Sholto is still alive?"

"Why, *of course!*" exclaimed the old man, gazing at him in astonishment. "Do *you* not think so?"

"Yes, I do," Rye said breathlessly. "But the Warden —"

"Oh, the *Warden!*" Tallus flapped his hands contemptuously, the knifepoint missing Rye's arm by a hairbreadth.

"I — I am sure that Dirk — my other brother — is still alive, too," Rye stammered. "I do not know why I am so certain, but . . ."

"I daresay you can feel it, if you were fond of him," the healer said vaguely, his eyes straying back to the skimmer on the table. "You and I are two of a kind. I knew it the first moment I saw you years ago. Sholto jeers at the idea, of course. Poor Sholto believes in nothing he cannot see."

He tore his eyes away from the skimmer and looked back at Rye. "So — both your brothers are out there, beyond the Wall. And you plan to go and find them. Is that it?"

Rye's breath caught in his throat. He gaped at the healer, unable to speak.

"If you have come to ask my opinion, I believe it is an excellent idea," Tallus said, nodding vigorously. "I had not realized how you had grown, or I would have come to you to suggest it. I thought of going after Sholto myself, of course, but I hesitated to leave Southwall without a healer. Not to mention that it is unlikely a limping old man could do a pinch of good out there in the wilds."

He clapped Rye on the shoulder. "But you, my boy, are a different matter. Go, with all speed! My thoughts will be with you."

Rye swallowed and found his voice. "No! Healer Tallus, that is not why I came. I cannot go beyond the Wall! I am too young. And even if I were of age, I could not leave Mother alone."

Tallus's eyebrows shot up, and his mouth turned down at the corners.

"Indeed!" he growled. "Then why are you here?"

"I — I need to make more skimmer repellent," Rye stammered. "So we have supplies for next season. I have Sholto's recipe, but the ingredients —"

"Nonsense!" Tallus snapped, shaking his head

irritably. "You could have come on the day of rest to ask me about that! Why hurry here today?"

Rye wet his lips. "I — I felt I could not wait," he said feebly.

"Exactly!" Tallus cried. "You were drawn here because something in you knew I would understand you. Face it, boy! Stop deceiving yourself!"

"Healer Tallus, I cannot go beyond the Wall!" Rye almost shouted. "They would not let me!"

Tallus grinned at him, put down his knife, and drew on heavy gloves.

"Go and find your brothers, young Rye," he said, picking up the knife again and bending over the skimmer. "You are young and strong, and your hair is as red as ever. You are just the man for the task. And it is what you want, even if you do not know it."

"But —"

"I think you should go quite soon," the old man went on without looking up. "Dirk and Sholto are alive for now, but plainly they are in danger. The very fact that you have come to me today is proof of that. Now be off with you!"

His mind in turmoil, Rye escaped from the evil-smelling room and ran from the house.

FATE

Fate is strange, and our destinies can be shaped by very small decisions. If Rye had simply run home by the shortest way after leaving the healer's house, the whole course of his life might have been very different. Possibly, as time passed, he would have been able to push Tallus's disturbing words to the back of his mind and continue as before.

But he did not go home by the shortest way. Instead, upset and confused, he obeyed a sudden impulse to go home the long way, along the path beside the Wall trench.

Turning down the side road that led to the Wall path, passing houses reduced to rubble by skimmers, Rye told himself that it was sensible to avoid streets that by now would be thronged with people who would wonder why he was not at school.

But as he reached the path itself, and the Wall loomed before him, rising sheer into the clouds from the cavernous trench, he faced the truth. The Wall itself had drawn him.

The Wall of Weld had always been part of Rye's life, yet now he gazed at it as if he had never seen it before. He stared, transfixed, at the workers swarming over the scaffold that crisscrossed the lower sections of the smooth, mud-brick surface.

They reminded him of bees crawling over a frame in one of Lisbeth's beehives. They were so many that it was hard to see exactly what each one was doing. But each, Rye knew, had a special task and did it diligently, for the sake of Weld.

For the sake of the hive, Rye thought. And he stopped and looked back the way he had come, past the ruins of the side street, toward the row upon row of small, identical houses that stretched away from the trench as far as the eye could see.

He imagined the thousands of dutiful citizens working in and around those little houses, cleaning, mending, making, building, gathering food, caring for their young, without a thought of what might lie beyond their Wall. And again he thought of bees.

Then a faint sound broke through his thoughts. It was a tiny, piteous bleat — the sound of a very young creature in trouble.

If Rye had not been standing still, thinking about bees, he might have missed hearing the sound.

But he did hear it. And Rye was not one who could ignore the cry of a creature in distress.

So it was that he went searching. And so it was that at last he found, in a hole covered by a heap of rubble in one of the ruined houses, a baby goat. Somehow this baby alone had survived a skimmer attack that had wiped out its owners and its family. The stinking goat bones that lay scattered among the shattered bricks showed only too plainly what had happened to its mother and father.

When Rye had pulled away the rubble and lifted the little creature free, it bleated, and butted feebly at his chest. It had clearly been trapped for many days. It was very weak and almost dead of hunger and thirst.

The need to save it drove everything else from Rye's mind. He found an old washing basket among the ruins and put the goat gently inside it. Then, clutching his burden, he made for home.

The goat was small, but Rye's arms were aching by the time he pushed through the gate into his own back garden.

The bees were humming around their hives, and the bell tree's lowest branches hung almost to the ground, weighed down by ripening fruit. Gratefully, Rye left the basket in the shade of the tree and let himself into the deserted house. Weld doors were never locked in the daytime. A locked door was, in fact, a shameful thing, because it was a sign that the householders had secrets to keep or did not trust their neighbors.

It took no time at all for Rye to warm some goat's milk. It took much longer to coax the little goat to suck the milk, first from his fingers and then from a clean rag dipped into the bowl.

Only when all the milk was gone and the little animal had fallen asleep in its basket did Rye realize how tired he was. He left the basket where it was and went into the house.

The citizens of Weld did not sleep in the daytime unless they were very young, very old, or suffering from an illness, but Rye had had an almost sleepless night and an exhausting morning. The house was empty. There was no one to see what he did.

The urge to lie down on his bed was too strong to resist. He planned to close his eyes for just a little time, but the moment his head touched the pillow, he fell deeply asleep. And he did not wake.

If that day had been a day like any other, Lisbeth would have returned home from the square in the early afternoon. In skimmer season, most shoppers bought what they needed in the mornings. The afternoons were very slow, and most of the stallholders left the square not long after lunch.

But on this particular day, after she had closed her stall, Lisbeth decided to go and visit Crell's mother, Ritta, before going home.

Why she did this, she could not afterward tell. Perhaps it was because she now wore two gold brooches, instead of one. Perhaps it was because she wanted to urge Ritta to rejoice that her son was safe, instead of feeling shamed because he had come creeping home. Perhaps she simply wanted to lose herself for a time in bittersweet memories of the days when Ritta's husband and hers worked together on the Wall, when Dirk, Sholto, Crell, and Joliffe were schoolboys together, and when life was safe and unchanging.

Whatever the cause, she spent a long time drinking tea and talking to Ritta. She only realized how much time had slipped by when the end-of-work bell sounded. So it was that she hurried home very late, as the light began to fade. So it was that she burst through the front door very flurried, shouting for Rye, calling that they must seal the house quickly, quickly!

And Rye, woken with a shock from a sleep fathoms deep, leaped from his bed and ran to help her, still half caught in a vivid dream of Dirk peering down into a dark pit of stone.

He worked automatically, doing what he had done so often. His head felt as if it were stuffed with rags, but his hands knew what to do.

The house was secured just in time. His heart thudding, his hands stinking of skimmer repellent, Rye sank down at the table. Even now, the last shreds of his dream clouded his mind like spiderweb.

Only when the first flapping sounds of the skimmers began did he remember the baby goat in its basket beneath the bell tree.

With a thrill of horror, he heard a high, terrified bleating begin in the back garden.

"What is that?" Lisbeth hissed, turning from the fireplace. "What —?"

She froze as the sounds above the house abruptly ceased. It was as if the skimmers had suddenly paused in midair. There was a split second of silence pierced by another single plaintive bleat. And then there was a mighty flapping rush, and the awful sound of branches splintering under a great weight.

The little goat's cries stopped almost at once. But having tasted blood, the skimmers began searching for more. In terror, Rye and Lisbeth clung together as claws raked the shutters of the little house, and bodies thudded like giant fists against the door.

The locks held. The rags soaked in skimmer repellent sealed every gap. Try as they might, the skimmers could not enter the house. But their frenzy became no less, and outside, in the garden, the sounds of tearing and smashing went on, and on, and on.

In the morning, Rye and Lisbeth opened their door on ruin. The bell tree was nothing but a jagged stump. Torn branches, the bright leaves already limp and fading, lay on the ground in a litter of gnawed golden fruit and fragile goat bones, picked clean.

The beehives had been reduced to splinters. A few bees that had survived the attack crawled aimlessly among the broken roots of the shredded honey hedge. Rye knew they would soon die. They could not live without their hive.

A burning lump rose in his throat. He wanted to cover his eyes, to block out the terrible sight. But he made himself look. He had to look.

He had done this. He had brought the poor, doomed little goat home. He had left it, forgotten, under the bell tree, to cry out and attract the skimmers.

He would have given anything — anything — to turn back the clock. But what was done could not be undone.

Hardly knowing what he was doing, he began trying to move a branch that was blocking the path to the back gate.

"Leave it, Rye," Lisbeth said quietly.

She went back into the house. When Rye followed her, he saw that she was calmly making tea.

He could not speak to her. Over and over again, during the long night, he had said that he was sorry. There was no point in saying it all again. Yet what else did he have to say?

Lisbeth poured tea into two cups and set them on the table. Then she sat down, glanced at Rye, and patted the bench beside her, inviting him to join her.

"Rye, you are not to blame yourself anymore for this," she said. "Your warm heart led you to it, and your warm heart is what I love in you."

"I should not have slept," Rye whispered. "I should not have forgotten. Dirk would not have forgotten. Sholto would not."

"Perhaps." His mother's lips tightened. "But Dirk and Sholto are not here. Since they . . . went away, you have shouldered burdens that a boy your age should not have had to bear. You have shouldered them bravely, Rye. We have managed, alone together here, though we have had little enough. But now . . ."

For the first time, her voice trembled. She cleared her throat impatiently and went on.

"But now everything has changed. The beehives and the bell tree were our livelihood. Now they are gone."

"I can work, Mother," Rye said quickly. "I can work on the Wall!"

Lisbeth shook her head. "You are too young to work on the Wall, Rye. Even if you were not, the pay of a Wall apprentice would not be enough to support us. And there is no work for me here. No one in Southwall can afford to pay someone else to clean or cook for them these days."

Rye stared at her helplessly. She was gazing down at her cup. Her hands were clasped tightly around it, as if for warmth.

"And the skimmers will be back," she murmured. "Now they have tasted blood here, they will be back."

"So what are we going to do?" Rye asked in a small voice. He had the sinking feeling that he knew.

Lisbeth shrugged. "It is part of the Warden's duty to give work and shelter to citizens in need. So we will do what many others have been forced to do before us. We will go to the Keep."

THE KEEP

A few days later, Rye and Lisbeth left the little house in Southwall, taking with them only what they could carry on their backs. Their neighbors watched them go. Some wept a little. Others stared listlessly, too numbed by trials and tiredness to feel very much at all.

Lisbeth had used the last of their coins to pay for seats on the cart that carried passengers to the Keep.

"We could save the money and walk," she told Rye. "But I have heard that the best jobs are given to those who look tidy and clean when they arrive. Besides, if we have no money at all in our pockets, it will be clearly seen that we are in real need."

She spoke briskly — even cheerfully. But there was a new hardness in her eyes that made her seem almost like someone Rye did not know.

The cart, smartly painted with yellow and gray

stripes, was drawn by six plump Weld goats and driven by a woman in a yellow uniform and peaked cap. Rye had always thought that to ride in it would be a great adventure. He had always envied its passengers when he saw it setting off from the town square.

But after half a day of smooth traveling along the broad, straight road, squeezed between his silent mother and an old Eastwall man who quickly went to sleep, he grew bored and restless.

There was nothing to see but square fields, clipped hedges, skimmer traps, trees rigidly pruned to the legal height, and signs — many, many signs giving information, warnings, and advice to travelers.

The signs reminded Rye of Dirk. The memory of Dirk reminded him of where this journey was going to end.

The Keep.

One step closer, he caught himself thinking. He glanced quickly at his mother, as if somehow she might have sensed his thoughts. But Lisbeth was staring into space, rocking slightly with the movement of the cart.

Rye looked down at the bundle of clothes pressed against his knees. A smooth, sturdy stick was threaded under one of the bundle's fastening straps. It was a stick from the ravaged bell tree. He had picked it up and carried it away with him out of his need to keep some remembrance, some small part of home.

Only now did it occur to him that it could be a weapon.

He slid the stick from beneath the strap and felt its weight. He felt how well it fit into his hand. A nervous fluttering began in his stomach.

Do not think of it, he told himself. *They will not let you go. You are too young.*

He thought the same that night as he lay trying to get to sleep in the small, hot room of the roadside inn at which the cart had stopped just before sunset. And waking at dawn, hearing his mother turn restlessly in her narrow bed on the other side of the room, he berated himself for even thinking of leaving her alone, for any reason.

You are all she has left, he thought. *The Warden would never allow you to be separated.*

But about this, at least, he was to find that he was quite wrong.

They arrived at the Keep when the sun was high in the milky sky. The ancient fortress bulged from the Wall like a blister of stone. Towering over the little houses of Westwall, it looked exactly like the pictures Rye had seen of it, right down to the two huge brown animals standing on either side of the gateway with Keep soldiers perched on their backs.

"Mother, look!" Rye whispered in awe. "Look at the horses!"

But Lisbeth had seen the famous Keep horses as a girl and could not spare a glance for them now. She was carefully reading the sign that stood before the gateway.

WELCOME TO THE KEEP OF WELD

RAISED BY WELD'S FOUNDER, THE GREAT SORCERER DANN, THE KEEP IS THE LARGEST AND MOST ANCIENT BUILDING IN WELD. IT IS MADE ENTIRELY OF STONE, AND THE WALL OF WELD ITSELF FORMS PART OF ITS CONSTRUCTION.

THE KEEP IS THE CENTER OF WELD GOVERNMENT. IT IS HOME TO THE WARDEN OF WELD AND HIS HOUSEHOLD. IT ALSO HOUSES THE WELD ARMY AND THE FAMOUS KEEP HORSES. IN RECENT YEARS, THE KEEP HAS PROVIDED CARE AND SHELTER TO THE HOMELESS CHILDREN POPULARLY KNOWN AS "KEEP ORPHANS."

VISITORS ARE ASKED NOT TO STRAY BEYOND THE PUBLIC COURTYARD.

CITIZENS SEEKING INFORMATION, AID, OR ADVICE SHOULD APPLY AT THE DOOR MARKED "INFORMATION."

VOLUNTEERS FOR THE WARDEN'S QUEST SHOULD APPLY AT THE DOOR MARKED "VOLUNTEERS."

The great paved courtyard was a confusion of people. Some were rushing about importantly with folders under their arms. Most seemed to be standing in line or just milling around aimlessly. Children clad in shabby red — the "Keep orphans," no doubt — ran in and out, looking very much at home.

In the center of the courtyard was a bell tree, very old and gnarled and bearing only a few dry, speckled fruit. A fence of metal railings surrounded it. The label on the railings read:

> "THE SORCERER'S TREE"
> THIS RARE BELL TREE WAS PLANTED BY
> DANN HIMSELF TO CELEBRATE THE
> COMPLETION OF THE KEEP.
> PLEASE DO NOT TOUCH.

Lisbeth and Rye turned away from the tree, their hearts aching with sad memories of home. In silence, they joined the other needy citizens standing in line before the door marked "Information." The line was long and moved slowly.

When at last they reached the pleasant-faced woman at the desk beyond the door, Lisbeth told their story and showed the two gold badges.

The woman filled in a form while they waited in silence. Then she filled in another. When she had finished, she looked up brightly and told Lisbeth that she could have work in the Keep kitchens and a bed in the women's dormitory. Rye would be sent to Welds Center to work in the fields.

"The Center!" Lisbeth gasped, drawing Rye closer to her. "But surely . . . surely we can stay together?"

"Sadly, that is impossible," the woman said briskly, smiling and shaking her head. "There is no suitable work for your son in the Keep. But do not fear. He will have all the care and discipline he needs in the boys' camp in the Center. It will be the making of him!"

"If Rye goes to the Center, I must go there, too," Lisbeth said.

The woman behind the desk suppressed a sigh. Her smile stayed in place, but Rye could feel her irritation.

"There is no work for you in the Center, Citizen," she said patiently. "You must understand that we do our best to help all those in need, but they cannot be a burden to others. They must work for their keep."

"I know that!" Lisbeth cried, color mounting on her cheeks. "We are very willing to work, but —"

The woman's voice hardened, very slightly. "Did you not say you had no means to support yourself and your son, Citizen?" she asked, tapping her fingers on the forms she had just completed.

"Yes," Lisbeth breathed. "But —"

"Then there is no more to be said."

And it seemed there was not. The woman gave them a few moments for a tearful farewell. Then a Keep orphan was summoned to guide Lisbeth to the kitchens, and Rye was given his own form to deliver to the duty guard in the courtyard. A group marching to the Center was to set off that very afternoon, it seemed.

But Rye went nowhere near the duty guard. Instead, he lined up for the public lavatories. When he was safely inside a cubicle, he tore the form into tiny pieces and disposed of it.

Then he washed his face and hands, shouldered his bundle, and crossed the courtyard to the door marked "Volunteers."

❊

Rye had expected that it would be difficult to get what he wanted, but he found the task was strangely easy. All he had to do was lie.

Normally, this would have been hard for him. Like most Weld citizens, he was usually very truthful. But the helpless anger roused in him by the smiling woman at the Information desk seemed to have burned away his finer feelings. He did not even change color as he told the man at the Volunteers desk that he had just turned eighteen.

The man, who had very little hair on his head and had tried to make up for it by growing an enormous gray mustache, had clearly been very bored before Rye came in. He was delighted to have someone to talk to.

He insisted that Rye take a glass of barley water with him while he filled in the application form, saying that Rye was the first volunteer he had seen for months. On hearing Rye's lie, he looked him up and down and merely commented that he was a little small for his age. But then, he said, he had often heard that people with red hair tended to be puny.

Rye merely smiled and nodded.

In no time at all, he was being led through a maze of corridors and into a dim waiting room. Comfortable armchairs lined the room's walls. In the center, there was a polished table on which stood a large carved chest, a pen, and a crystal inkwell.

Rye's guide presented him with a small, flat box which he said contained volunteers' supplies, wished him luck, and regretfully left him, telling him that the Warden would be along presently.

Having stowed his supplies in his bundle, Rye began to prowl the room nervously.

The Warden! He had not expected that he would have to face the Warden in person.

He paced past the yawning fireplace, which was dusty with ash. He circled the table, peering at the carved chest. He twitched aside a red velvet curtain to reveal not a window, but a small padlocked door. Then he had the strong feeling that he was being watched.

He dropped the curtain as if it had stung him, and went to stand beside the table.

He thought of what Dirk had always said about the Warden being just an ordinary man, and a timid, stupid one at that. This calmed him a little, but not enough to allow him to stand still. When a door snapped open on the far side of the room, he nearly jumped out of his skin.

A very handsome, dark-haired young woman looked around the door, quickly surveyed the room, and frowned.

"Lyon is not here!" she snapped to someone behind her.

"He must have gone to his meal, then, ma'am," a deep male voice answered meekly. "He *was* there, I am sure!"

"Filling the inkwell, he was," another man put in.

The young woman clicked her tongue. She pulled back her head, not bothering to shut the door.

"It is not good enough!" Rye heard her exclaim. "I ordered a new sketchbook *two days* ago! Lyon promised faithfully to bring it this morning. It is outrageous that the Warden's daughter should have to beg for her needs. See to it at once!"

Rye made a face. If this was the Warden's daughter, it was no wonder the Warden kept her out of public view. She would make a very uncomfortable wife.

"Yes, ma'am," the deep voice muttered. "Sorry, ma'am."

"Sorry, ma'am," the other man echoed.

There was an impatient snort and the sound of rustling silk. A door slammed.

"Why should I run her messages?" grumbled the man with the deep voice. "Do I look like a lady's maid? It is time someone told her that Keep soldiers work for the Warden of Weld, not his useless daughter!"

"Shh!" his companion hissed.

A door creaked. Two pairs of heels snapped smartly together.

"At ease, men," a rather hesitant, mumbling voice said. "And how are you both today?"

"Very well, Warden, sir," the two men replied together.

"Good, very good," the newcomer said. "Now, I understand we have a new volunteer — the first for quite a while. Quite a surprise! Dear me, yes! I will just go and . . ."

Rye heard shuffling footsteps. He stepped back a little.

A plump man wearing the Warden's traditional long red robe came into the room. He had a mild, slightly vacant-looking face with sagging cheeks and watery blue eyes. He was clutching a large sheet of paper in his stubby fingers.

He stopped abruptly when he caught sight of Rye. His mouth fell open a little, and his eyes bulged. Rye stood up very straight, making himself look as tall as possible, and held his breath.

But the Warden's hesitation, whatever its cause, did not last. He recovered himself almost immediately and bustled forward again.

"Ah!" he said. "Greetings, Volunteer!"

And now it was Rye's turn to stare. The Warden looked only vaguely like the official portrait that hung on the schoolhouse wall. In the portrait, he was younger and slimmer, his chin looked firmer, his hair was browner and thicker, and his eyes were bluer. Also, in the painting, the Warden was mounted on a Keep horse, which made him look far more important.

In some confusion, Rye realized that the Warden was waiting expectantly, his sparse eyebrows slightly raised.

Hurriedly, Rye bowed. The bow felt clumsy, but it seemed to satisfy the Warden, for he nodded, shuffled forward, and put the paper down on the polished table.

"This is your Volunteer Statement," he said, taking up the pen and dipping it fussily into the ink. "Read it very carefully before you sign. You can still change your mind at this point, and no harm done. But once you have signed, there is no turning back."

THE CHAMBER
OF THE DOORS

R ye crept to the table, took the pen the Warden was holding out to him, and looked down at the paper.

VOLUNTEER STATEMENT

• I HEREBY DECLARE that I am of age, and that I am leaving the safety of Weld of my own free will.

• I UNDERSTAND that once I am beyond the Wall, the Warden of Weld cannot be held responsible for any harm that may come to me.

• I AGREE that if I do not return to the city within one year and one day, I shall be officially regarded as lost.

• I SWEAR that beyond the Wall I will not admit to being a citizen of Weld, even under the threat of death.

Signed

Wondering if this document was what had made Crell discover that his ankle was injured, Rye set his lips and signed.

The Warden sighed, picked up the paper, blew on it to dry the ink, and put it carefully into the carved box, which seemed to contain many other signed papers exactly like it.

No doubt Dirk's statement is in there, Rye thought. And Sholto's.

"Very well, Rye," the Warden said, closing the lid of the box. "Collect your belongings and follow me."

He led the way to the curtain covering the padlocked door, pulled the red velvet aside, and drew out a small key.

"Is this the secret way?" Rye asked.

The Warden frowned and shook his head. He removed the padlock and opened the door to reveal a steep, narrow stone stairway that spiraled down into darkness.

As he ushered Rye through the doorway, torches fixed to the stone walls sprang into life, flooding the stairs with dancing light.

Dann's magic, Rye thought, his skin prickling.

Clever tricks, he seemed to hear Sholto jeering in his mind. But if this was a trick, it was impossible to see how it had been done. He was sure the Warden had touched nothing.

"Hold tightly to the safety rail, Volunteer," the

Warden advised, shutting the door behind them. "These steps are old and very dangerous."

Despite himself, Rye had to smile. Steep steps were surely the least of his problems, considering the peril he was about to face.

The Warden must have noticed the smile, because he drew himself up and looked stern.

"While you are still in Weld, you are still under my care," he said stiffly. "Down you go, then. Right to the bottom, if you please."

Gripping the rail, Rye began to go down the steps. The Warden followed, his soft shoes making faint brushing sounds on the stone.

Down they went, and down. The air grew heavy with the odors of damp and mold. Rye seemed to feel the whole weight of the Keep pressing down upon him.

His skin prickled more and more. He grew increasingly uneasy and his steps slowed.

"Keep moving, Volunteer," said the Warden behind him.

"What is this place, Warden?" Rye could not help asking. "Where are we?"

"Below the ground," the Warden said. "We are moving into the base of the Keep — the oldest place in Weld. Keep moving. There is not much farther to go."

He sounded quite placid. The atmosphere of the stairway had not affected him at all, it seemed.

Rye forced himself to move on. With every step, it seemed harder to breathe. Then, just when he felt he was going to have to stop, he saw a flash from below.

"There," said the Warden.

Just moments later, Rye was stumbling over the last step into a small, glittering, circular room. He blinked, trying to adjust to the sudden, brilliant light. Whatever he had been expecting, it was not this.

The ceiling of the little room was bright, dreamlike blue, shining like glass lit from within. Thousands of tiny tiles, vivid as precious gems, made swirling patterns of red, yellow, green, and white on the floor and walls.

It was like being inside a jewel box buried deep within the rock. Rye stood staring, awed by the beauty and the strangeness.

Straight ahead of him, two soldiers holding tall spears stood on either side of a carved gold medallion fixed to the wall. On seeing Rye, they tilted their spears so that the shafts of the weapons crossed protectively over the golden disc.

"I bring a volunteer," said the Warden formally. "He has signed the Statement and may enter the chamber."

Without changing expression, the soldiers uncrossed their spears and stood back in their places.

"Approach the wall, Volunteer," the Warden said to Rye. "Place the palm of your left hand upon the Sign of Dann, and you will gain entrance to the chamber from which you can leave the city. Once inside the chamber, use the same hand to make your choice."

"Choice?" Rye repeated in confusion.

"You will see," said the Warden, and stepped back.

Slowly, Rye approached the medallion. He felt as if he were in a waking dream.

I am about to leave Weld, he thought, trying to make himself believe it.

He looked for the outline of a door around the medallion but could see nothing. The glittering tiles swept in unbroken lines around the room, lines that had no beginning and no end. Rye's eyes dazzled.

Blinking, he turned his attention to the soldiers flanking the medallion. He wondered if they had been on duty the day Dirk stood in this spot, or the day Sholto came down those dark, winding steps with the Warden of Weld padding behind.

He would have liked to ask. But the soldiers stood at attention, staring straight over his head. He knew they would not speak.

He peered at the medallion's carved surface. He saw that what he had taken to be simple decoration was actually a large letter *D* entwined with leaves and flowers. The flowers looked exactly like the badges his mother had received in honor of Dirk and Sholto, and suddenly, Rye realized that they were bell tree blooms. Dimly, he wondered why he had not noticed this before.

He raised his left hand. He saw that it was trembling, and struggled to hold it still.

How would Dirk have felt at this moment? Excited, of course — full of energy and fire. And Sholto? Sholto would have been all fascinated curiosity. Having come this far, neither of them would have hesitated.

Rye pressed his palm against the medallion.

A hot, tingling sensation ran up his arm all the way to the shoulder. Pinpoints of light exploded before his eyes. He heard himself yell with shock.

And then, somehow, he was no longer in the little tiled room. He was in a much larger space — somewhere bare and dim, still faintly echoing with the last traces of his cry.

His head spinning, Rye swung around to look behind him. There was only a plain stone wall. Hardly able to believe it was real, he stretched out his hand to touch it. It was cold and solid under his fingertips. He looked down and saw dusty rock under his feet.

Taking a deep breath to steady himself, he slipped the bell tree stick from his bundle. Gripping the stick tightly, he turned around again.

He was in a large stone chamber. A huge old fireplace gaped on the wall to his right. The wall to his left was entirely bare. In the wall directly in front of him were three Doors.

The Doors stood side by side. One was gold, one

was silver, and one was plain, heavy wood bound with brass.

The golden Door was magnificent — richly carved with the likenesses of fantastic beasts. The silver Door was elegant, smoothly patterned with mysterious pictures, signs, and symbols. The wooden Door, made of planks far broader than any Rye had ever seen, bore no decoration at all except the brass studs and bands that made it strong.

Words had been engraved on the stone above the Doors. Rye moved closer so he could read them.

THREE MAGIC DOORS YOU HERE BEHOLD
TIME TO CHOOSE: WOOD? SILVER? GOLD?
LISTEN TO YOUR INNER VOICE
AND YOU WILL MAKE THE WISEST CHOICE.

Rye glanced from one Door to another. He knew at once that the wooden Door appealed to him the most. Unlike the other two Doors, it did not seem out of place against the rough stone in which it was set. It was plain and without ornament, yet to him it was beautiful, because it was so ancient and so well crafted.

He jumped violently as he heard a scrabbling sound behind him. He whirled around.

A cloud of ash was billowing from the fireplace. As Rye gaped in amazement, a scrawny girl, covered in soot from head to foot, crawled out of the cloud and slid onto the stone floor of the chamber.

Pulling down the scarf that had covered her mouth and nose, the girl jumped to her feet. Her garments, the red trousers and tunic of a Keep orphan, were tattered and much too big for her. A bulging cloth bag hung at her waist, suspended by a belt of plaited rope. She was wearing what looked like filthy bedroom slippers, and a helmet-shaped red cap covered her head completely.

Before Rye could move, she sprang at him and seized his arm.

"Take me with you, Rye!" she hissed in his ear.

Astounded, Rye tried to push her away, but she clung to him like an attacking skimmer, her nails biting through the sleeve of his jacket.

"I will not hinder you, I swear!" she whispered. "Once we are on the other side of the Wall, I will go my way and you can go yours. Just take me through a Door — any Door you choose. I cannot do it alone. The Doors will open only for those who have touched the Sign of Dann, and I cannot get to the Sign. It is too well guarded."

"But why do *you* want to go through the Wall?" Rye cried.

"That is my affair!" the girl panted. "Just make up your mind that I am going to do it. All the other volunteers refused me, but I will not let you do so. You may be my last chance!"

"No!" Rye gasped. "Get away!"

The girl gritted her teeth. "You must do as I say," she insisted. "You will do as I say, or I will report you for signing a false Statement!"

"*What?*" Furious, Rye again tried to shake his attacker off. She merely tightened her grip and hung on. She was very much stronger than she looked.

"You swore that you were of age, but you are not!" she hissed. "I heard your mother talking to another worker in the kitchens. She said her son, Rye, was only sixteen, and had been sent to the Center. *Then* I saw you with the Warden, signing the Volunteer Statement. You have lied your way into the Chamber of the Doors!"

Rye remembered the fallen ash in the fireplace of the waiting room. He remembered the feeling of being watched.

"Leave me alone!" he shouted, struggling to free himself.

"I will tell!" the girl threatened. "You deceived the Warden. You signed a false oath. Your name will be disgraced! Your *mother's* name will be disgraced! She will never be able to hold up her head again. She may even be turned out of the Keep to starve!"

"The Warden would not do that!" panted Rye.

"How do you know?" the girl spat. "Will you risk it?"

Rye knew he could not. Abruptly, he stopped struggling. Anger still raged within him, but now it was ice-cold instead of hot.

"You are mad," he muttered.

The girl's lip curled. "And you are a liar. A boy pretending to be a man. A boy armed with a stick, who dreams of becoming Warden of Weld!"

"I do not —" Rye began hotly, then broke off, biting his tongue. What did this odious girl's taunts matter to him? If he was leaving Weld only to find his brothers, that was his concern, and his alone. He was not going to explain himself to her.

He turned quickly to face the Doors, dragging the girl with him. With satisfaction, he heard her catch her breath. So, now that she had what she thought she wanted, she was afraid. He was glad — very glad.

"I advise you to let me go," he said coldly. "This is your last chance to save yourself."

The girl said nothing but still gripped his arm as if afraid he would try to shake her off at the last moment. He put her out of his mind, only vaguely aware that she was keeping pace with him as he approached the Doors and surveyed them one by one.

Gold. Silver. Wood. Again, Rye's gaze lingered on the last Door. He looked up at the words written above it in stone.

LISTEN TO YOUR INNER VOICE
AND YOU WILL MAKE THE WISEST CHOICE.

But I am not here to choose for myself, Rye thought, and felt a pang of regret as he turned away from the wooden Door.

He knew that Dirk and Sholto would not have felt the same as he did.

He knew without a doubt that Dirk would have chosen the golden Door — the Door fit for kings and heroes. And, almost certainly, Sholto would have chosen the silver Door — the elegant door of knowledge, puzzles, and secrets.

So if Rye was to do what he had set out to do, it was a choice between those two. And in fact, if his family was ever to be united again, there was no choice at all.

Dirk was the eldest brother. Dirk was a hero and a leader. Dirk had become the family's protector and strength after his father's death. If Dirk could be found and brought home, he would be able to save them all.

Rye stepped forward. As he stretched out his left hand toward the golden Door, he heard the orphan girl sigh.

He had almost forgotten she was there. And there was no time to think of her now. The next instant, his hand had closed on the vast gold doorknob, the door was creaking open to reveal a shining, colorless space, and he was being jerked forward, sucked off his feet, into emptiness.

THE FELL ZONE

When Rye came to himself, he at first thought he was dreaming. He was lying on his back, his bell tree stick still gripped in his hand. There was a strange, sharp smell in the air, and a whispering voice somewhere very near.

The first sign . . . do you see?

Rye's eyes flew open. High above him, huge tree branches thick with rustling leaves were swaying like the flailing limbs of some great, shaggy beast. The sight was so unnatural, so terrifying, that at first Rye could not move a finger. Then a word Sholto had taught him came into his mind.

Wind.

Wind was a thing that existed beyond the Wall and in the skies above it. It was like the evening breezes that sometimes stirred the still air of Weld but much, much stronger. It was wind that sometimes blew dark rain clouds over Weld, then whisked them away again after the rain had fallen. The same wind beat on the unprotected coast of Dorne and drove the ships that sailed the Sea of Serpents.

It was wind that was making the treetops move.

And the trees were giants because their roots were not confined in clay pots like Weld trees, and their branches were not pruned to the proper size each year. They were wild trees, which had been allowed to grow and spread till they became monsters.

I am beyond the Wall, Rye thought. Cautiously he sat up, and the stick fell from his hand as he instinctively crossed his fingers and his wrists.

He could see great rocks that in Weld would be priceless treasure. He could see untidy drifts of overgrown bushes and the countless trunks of untamed trees. Fallen branches lay everywhere, the precious wood tangled with rampant vines, and covered in fungus, left to rot.

Dead leaves blanketed the ground. No one had raked them up to make compost that would help crops to grow. They just lay there, decaying where they had fallen, going to waste like the wood, feeding the monstrous trees.

There were no roads or paths. There were no signs giving directions or warning of dangers. Except for the rustling of the swaying treetops, there was no sound.

No sound of digging or hammering. No sound of

cart wheels rumbling. No voices calling, singing, or chattering. No bells.

No human sounds at all. But Rye had a growing sense of hostile life silently watching, waiting. . . .

Abruptly he twisted to look behind him. His stomach turned over.

The golden Door was not there. The Wall of Weld was not there.

Nothing was there but more towering rocks, more straggling bushes, more trees.

Sweat broke out on Rye's forehead. His legs tingled with the urge to leap up and run, run wildly, searching for the Door.

Panic kills, he seemed to hear Dirk whispering in his ear. *I have seen it so often, on the Wall. When disaster strikes, workers who keep their heads have a far better chance of survival than those who do not.*

Rye gritted his teeth and turned slowly away from the place where the Door should have been. Pressing his crossed wrists firmly against his chest, he forced himself to remain still, trying to fight down the fear.

He thought of the shining space he had glimpsed behind the golden Door just before he was pulled through it. Clearly, the Door was no ordinary door. It was a thing of ancient magic which did not obey the rules of the everyday world. Perhaps, for the safety of Weld, it delivered those who used it to a place well away from the Wall.

He was somewhere in the Fell Zone. He felt he could be sure of that. Perhaps it was because the place seemed so utterly barren of signs of human life. Perhaps it was because of the feeling of dread that was still making his skin crawl.

Rye pictured the map he had looked at every morning for so long. The Fell Zone was a band of land that encircled Weld. Just a narrow band. The giant trees hid the Door and the Wall from sight now, perhaps, but the trees could not go on forever. Once he was beyond them, the Wall, at least, would be clearly visible. Dirk would help him find the Door again. When he found Dirk . . . *if* he found Dirk . . .

His heart thudded sickeningly. Again panic rose in him.

Then his glazed eyes fell on the scruffy girl in red, lying not far from where he sat. His breath caught in his throat, and a sudden wave of relief surged through him. He had forgotten the girl — forgotten that he was not alone.

No sooner had this thought crossed his mind than relief was swamped by mingled irritation and shame. *That girl is no friend of yours*, he told himself angrily. *You do not want her company!*

But the fact was, just the sight of another human in this alien place had given him courage. He no longer felt the urge to run. Slowly he uncrossed his wrists, took hold of his stick, and stood up.

·The girl was curled up on her side, her hands clasped under her chin. Her eyes were closed.

Perhaps she was injured. Rye felt a sharp stab of unease but instantly suppressed it. The girl was not his responsibility. She had forced him to bring her here. He could not, *would* not, allow her to interfere with his search for Dirk.

Still, he could not leave her lying unprotected in the open, any more than he could have left the baby goat to die of thirst. He glanced around warily, then approached the girl and tapped her shoulder gently with his stick.

The girl's eyes opened. They were muddy brown with a green tinge, like the water that lay in the Wall trench after rain. She rolled onto her back and blinked up at Rye. Her pale lips moved.

"We are through?"

Rye nodded.

The eyes closed briefly, as if with relief. Then the girl struggled to her feet.

The second sign . . .

Rye jumped. The words had been soft as sighs, but he had heard them — he was sure he had heard them. Quickly he looked around, half fearing to see someone standing behind him.

There was no one there. Slowly, Rye turned back to face the girl.

She did not seem to have heard anything. As she straightened, Rye realized that she was not as young and scrawny as her ill-fitting garments and ugly cap made her look. In fact, though she was slender, she was as tall as he was.

He watched her take a deep breath, and then another. She shivered all over. Then she glanced around.

Rye waited for her to see there was no sign of the Door. He waited for her to show terror and cross her fingers and wrists. But she merely frowned and began fumbling with the knot of the scarf that still hung around her neck.

"I might have known the golden Door would send us straight into the Fell Zone," she muttered, pulling off the scarf and tying it to the nearest bush. "Any fool could see that it was a lure for those who fancy themselves as heroes. Most of the volunteers chose it. No doubt they are all dead by now."

Fear and rage shot through Rye like flame. "Hold your tongue!" he snapped.

The girl jerked back, blinking as if she had been slapped. Recovering herself, she tossed her head and set off through the trees, plowing through the dead leaves. In moments, she had disappeared into the undergrowth.

Rye told himself he was glad to see the end of her. Then, as his anger cooled, he began to change his mind.

Whatever he felt, his reason was telling him that for the present any companion, however disagreeable, must be better than none. The Fell Zone was a place of monsters. Sholto had been sure the skimmers bred there. Whether they did or not, it was clearly a fearsome place. If even the bloodthirsty barbarians of the coast would not enter it, its dangers must be many, and terrible.

And perhaps one of those dangers was watching Rye now — one or several. For he was sure he was being watched. He could feel it. His nerves were jumping under his skin.

But did it make sense to follow the girl, just for the sake of company? She had plunged into the wilderness without thought. Clearly she had no idea of where she was going.

The next moment, a piercing scream settled the matter. Rye did not hesitate. He snatched up his bundle and ran, following the scuffed trail in the fallen leaves.

Just past a monstrous vine thicket, he found the girl in red lying facedown on the ground.

"I tripped," she babbled, scrambling up and shaking off his hand as he tried to help her. "It was not my fault. There was something hard, hidden under the leaves, and I . . ."

Her voice trailed off as she saw Rye staring down, his face frozen.

The leaves that had covered the hidden object had been brushed away by her fall. A stone had been revealed — a smooth stone with words crudely scratched upon it.

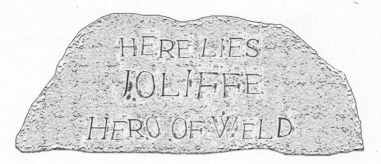

HERE LIES
JOLIFFE
HERO OF WELD

"Joliffe," Rye whispered, falling to his knees.

His heart seemed to twist in his chest. Rough as the scratchings were, he knew without doubt that it was Dirk who had laid Joliffe to rest.

Had Dirk simply come upon his friend lying dead? Or had they been together when . . . ?

"Did you know him?" The girl's voice seemed very faint. "Did you know this Joliffe? Was he a volunteer?"

Rye swallowed and nodded.

"I must have met him, then," the girl said huskily. "I tried to persuade every volunteer who entered the Chamber of the Doors to take me through the Wall."

Rye made no answer.

"I apologize. . . ." His companion cleared her throat. "I am sorry for what I said — about the volunteers who chose the golden Door. I meant . . . no disrespect."

"Yes you did," said Rye. He wiped his eyes with the back of his hand and got to his feet again.

The girl hesitated, as if she was about to say

something more, then seemed to decide there was no point. She turned and moved on, making no comment as Rye followed her, a few steps behind.

"Have you any idea where you are going?" Rye asked coldly.

The girl glanced at him over her shoulder. "I am just following the path," she said. "I could not think of a better plan."

Rye shook his head. There was no path that he could see. The girl was mad.

But still he followed her. Anything was better than being alone in this place.

After only a few moments, however, he knew that something was wrong. The walking was far too easy. Sweat broke out on his brow as he realized it was harder to slow down than to keep moving. An invisible force was drawing him on.

"Wait!" he shouted.

The girl stopped, skidding a little on the leaves. And it was only as she looked back in alarm, as she looked *up* at Rye, and he looked *down* at her, that he saw his mistake.

Sorcery had not been speeding their progress. Walking was rapid and easy because the ground on which they trod sloped downward!

Rye seemed to hear Sholto jeering in his ear.

Ignorant people often call things magic when they do not understand them.

Rye cursed himself for being so stupid. It was no

excuse that Weld was perfectly flat, and he had never walked down a hill in his life before. He was not in Weld now — he knew that! And the girl in red had not been deceived.

"What is it?" she called softly, looking nervously from side to side, then back at Rye.

"I . . ." He could not bring himself to explain. "I want to know your name," he finally burst out, snatching at the first question he could think of.

The girl folded her arms and pressed her lips together. It occurred to Rye that perhaps she clung to the old Weld belief that to know a person's name gave you power over that person. She was strange enough to believe anything.

"You know *my* name," he pointed out. "It is only fair that you should tell me yours."

"Sonia," she said at last. "My name is Sonia, if you must know."

She turned and hurried on.

The slope was becoming steeper. With every step, the rocks grew less, but the trees grew larger, and the bushes and vines more luxuriant. Ferns massed on the ground, splashing the fallen leaves with bright, tender green. Rye kept thinking he caught glimpses of movement from the corners of his eyes, but whenever he turned to look, he could see nothing.

Sonia wound her way quickly through the trees, occasionally hesitating before choosing one direction or another. At first, Rye could only trail after her blindly, but after a time, he found that he was able to guess which way she would go.

There *was* a path. The marks of it were very faint, but they were there. Once he had seen them, Rye could not understand why he had not noticed them before.

At least, he thought, *Sonia is not as mad as I thought, and we are not just wandering aimlessly. The path must lead somewhere.*

But where?

Rye forced that disturbing question out of his mind. For good or ill, he and Sonia really had no choice but to follow the path if they were to have any chance of living through the night. The rustling treetops hid the sky, but he knew that by now it must be dimming. Soon the sun would go down, and the skimmers would take flight. He and Sonia had to find shelter by then.

"We had better —" he began, then found himself crowding into Sonia as she stopped abruptly.

He saw what had halted her, and his blood ran cold.

Right across their path, strung between two trees, a slimy net sagged like a vast, crude spiderweb. And hanging in the web was the skeleton of a man, the bones picked clean.

Rye felt a roaring in his ears. His mind flew to Dirk, but almost at once, he realized that his fears were foolish. These pitiful remains were not Dirk's. The bones showed that in life the dead man would not have been much taller than Crell. And instead of a skimmer hook, a small hatchet lay half buried in leaves at the foot of the net.

"What has done this?" Rye whispered.

Sonia shuddered. She looked pale and sick.

"Who knows?" she muttered. "Some creature of the Fell Zone — one of the creatures stalking us now, no doubt. They are all around us. Can you not feel them?"

Rye nodded, his heart thudding. He felt breathless. Again he thought he caught a flicker of movement by the side of the path. He swung around with a gasp, his hand tightening on his stick, but still he saw nothing.

"We had better move on," he said. "Soon the sun will set. And the skimmers . . ."

"Skimmers!" Sonia made an impatient sound. "Are skimmers all you can think of? You are as obsessed with them as everyone else in Weld!"

"Of course I am!" snapped Rye. "Because of the skimmers, I have lost my home and everyone I love! As you have yourself, Sonia! Or have you been so long in the safety of the Keep that you have forgotten?"

Sonia paused. An expression that might have been shame crossed her face. Then, without another word, she stepped from the path to move around the slimy net and its hideous burden.

And instantly the tree on that side seemed to come alive. What looked like a thick section of mottled bark peeled away, revealing itself to Rye's horrified eyes as a huge, lizardlike beast, foul-smelling slime dripping from its snarling jaws.

DOWNSTREAM

The monster reared up on its hind legs and lunged at Sonia, its mottled tail lashing, a fan of spines and skin rising on the back of its neck. Sonia screamed and ducked, avoiding the snapping jaws by a hair, and ran for her life. The beast dropped to all fours and leaped after her, frighteningly fast.

Yelling in shock, Rye shrugged off his bundle, snatched up the dead man's hatchet, and gave chase.

Ahead he could see flashes of red as Sonia wove frantically between the trees below him. The gigantic lizard was hurtling after her, gaining on her every moment. At first, it looked weirdly like a huge piece of tree bark careering down the slope, but in moments, its knobbly, scaly skin had begun to change, quickly taking on the nutty brown color of the dead leaves. Soon it was visible only because it was moving.

Rye pounded after it, slipping and sliding,

keeping his feet by a miracle. His heart felt as if it were bursting in his chest. The hatchet was in his hand. If only he could get a clear line of sight, he could throw it. His aim was usually good — not as good as Dirk's, but good enough. Surely, even running, he could hit a target as large as this huge lizard. Injure it, at least. Delay it.

And then what? Then his only weapon would be the bell tree stick.

He could not think of that. He just had to keep running, waiting for the moment when . . .

He lost sight of Sonia behind a tangle of bushes. He could hear her sobbing gasps, but he could not see her. He could only see the beast, a surging, hissing mass of brown. For an instant, it was directly below him, but before he could hurl the hatchet, the creature had wheeled around the bushes and disappeared. Then, suddenly, Sonia burst into view again. She was glancing over her shoulder, her face twisted in terror.

The beast was right behind her. It was almost upon her. And ahead of her . . .

Rye went cold. "Sonia!" he bellowed. "In front of you! Beware!"

He saw Sonia's head jerk as she heard him. She looked blindly ahead but did not see what Rye could see so clearly — the slimy strands of another crude net stretched across her path.

In horror, Rye saw the red figure run straight into the net. In horror, he saw her fixed by the sticky, gleaming strings, struggling like a fly in a spiderweb. In terror, he saw a second monstrous, drooling lizard peel itself from the tree to which it had been clinging and lumber forward to claim its captured prize.

But the monster chasing Sonia was not willing to surrender its prey to a rival. Seeing the second lizard, it gave a harsh bellow and rose onto its hind legs, the fan of skin on the back of its neck deepening to bloodred.

The second lizard snarled and sprang. The next moment, the two beasts were locked in combat, biting, slashing, and hissing.

And so intent were they on destroying each other that Rye, reaching the place at last, was able to dart past them to the web in which Sonia was struggling.

Without the hatchet, he would never have been able to free her. The slimy, foul-smelling cords of the net stretched as he tore at them, sticking wherever they touched and threatening to trap him, too. But the hatchet, once he stopped panicking and thought to use it, sliced through the slimy strands like a knife cutting greasy string.

Pulling the girl free at last, he caught her around the waist and hurled himself sideways, tipping them both over a leafy bank that rose beside the tatters of the net. Together they tumbled down a steep ferny slope. There was nothing to stop them. Nothing they snatched at was firm enough to hold them. Yelling, they rolled and slid, down and down, until at last they lay, panting and shuddering, on the soft, damp earth of the valley floor.

The light was dim and green. The thrashing, hissing sounds of the monster battle floated down to Rye's ears. They mingled with other, closer, sounds. Sonia's sobbing breaths. The gurgling of running water. Birdcalls, clear and pure, chiming like tiny bells. A soft, breathy murmuring that might have been ferns stirring in a breeze, or something more sinister.

Rye closed his eyes and held himself very still, concentrating on the murmuring noise, trying to make out what it was. Something slithering beneath a blanket of leaves? Skimmers waking, stretching their leathery wings somewhere near? Or . . . could it be — could it possibly be — whispering voices?

The murmuring gradually separated itself into words.

He is the one.

The signs are not perfect.

The third test remains. We shall see. . . .

"Rye, wake up!" Sonia's anxious voice cut through the whispers, which vanished abruptly.

Rye opened his eyes. Sonia was crouched beside him, shaking his shoulder. He blinked at her blearily.

"We should get away from here." Sonia glanced nervously up toward the sound of the lizard battle. "The one that wins may come after us."

Rye nodded and scrambled painfully to his feet. He found that his ears had not been deceiving him in one way at least. He had been lying on the sandy bank of a fast-running stream. He stared, fascinated, at the clear, bubbling water. It was so strange to see water flowing freely, with no gutters to guide it.

The stream rippled and sang over a bed of small, round blue pebbles that seemed to wink at him like bright eyes.

On the other side of the stream, fern-choked land rose as steeply as the ground behind him did. It was as if he and Sonia had fallen into a deep fold in the earth. Rye's head swam as he looked up. Every bone in his body ached. His knees felt as if they were made of butter left too long out of the cool room. He knew he could not climb just yet.

Fortunately, Sonia appeared to feel the same. "I think we should go this way," she said, pointing along the stream to the left.

"I, too," said Rye, and wondered why he was so sure. Perhaps it was because the stream was running in that direction. It seemed right to follow the stream.

He looked around for the hatchet but was not surprised when he could not see it. He had lost his grip on it in that sliding tumble down the hill with Sonia, and it had stayed where it had fallen. Now it lay buried in ferns somewhere on that steep slope above him. He would never find it. Perhaps no one would ever find it again.

He had lost his bundle, too. It still lay by the first net, and he was certainly not going back for it. He would just have to do without spare clothes and the box of supplies.

But the stick, the bell tree stick, was at his feet. It, at least, had not deserted him. He picked it up, feeling its smooth, familiar weight in his hand.

Sonia was kneeling by the stream, reaching down into the water. When she scrambled up, her arm wet to the elbow, Rye saw that she had scooped up a handful of the blue pebbles.

She saw him watching her and raised her chin defiantly, as if he had questioned her. "I like them," she mumbled, pushing the wet pebbles into the pocket of her tunic. "And they might be useful."

"Indeed," Rye said politely.

A boy with a stick and a girl with a pocketful of stones, he thought as he turned to go. *What a fine pair of heroes we are, to be sure!*

They began to follow the stream, looking warily left and right. Neither of them spoke. Gradually the sounds of the lizard battle faded away behind them, and at last, all they could hear was the babbling of the water, the bell-like calls of the unseen birds, and their own plodding footsteps.

"I would be dead now, if it weren't for you," Sonia said suddenly. "Thank you for — for what you did."

Rye glanced at her. She was staring straight ahead and frowning, as if the words had been hard to say. No doubt she was annoyed because she had had to be saved.

"I am sure you would have done the same for me," he murmured, replying to the thanks in the usual Weld fashion, though in Sonia's case, he was not at all sure of any such thing. For all he knew, she would have left him struggling in the beast's net.

"Why did you want to leave Weld, Sonia?" he asked abruptly. "Surely being a Keep orphan cannot be so bad? Surely the Warden is kind to you?"

She snorted with mirthless laughter. "The Warden? I have not seen the Warden face-to-face more than three or four times in my life! But that is not the point. I did not leave Weld just because I was unhappy. I left for the same reason you and all the other volunteers did."

Rye blinked. "You — what?"

"I want to find the Enemy sending the skimmers and destroy him!" snapped Sonia. "I do not see why men only should have the chance to be the Warden's heir! There now! Have a good laugh at me, if you will!"

She quickened her pace and walked on ahead without waiting for an answer. Rye followed, wondering.

They came to a place where the stream vanished from sight, though they could still hear it gurgling underground. The earth beneath their feet was carpeted in thick green moss. The ferns around them were giants — the trunks tall, straight columns of furry brown, the great emerald fronds arching gracefully overhead making a delicate canopy of living green lace. It was like wandering through a deserted temple.

Never had Rye seen anything so strangely beautiful. Awestruck, he walked on, barely aware of Sonia ahead, lost in a dream of shadowy green.

He had no idea for how long he had walked when, slowly, it came to him that something had changed. It took a moment for him to realize what the change was.

The birdcalls had stopped.

Rye looked around dazedly. The light was dimmer and greener than it had been before. He knew that in the world above, the sun must be going down.

An icy trickle of fear ran down his spine.

"Sonia!" he called in a low voice.

The girl was standing motionless between the trunks of two giant ferns that stood like sentinels not far ahead. She made no sign that she had heard him, but at least she had stopped moving.

Rye ran to catch up with her, blessing the soft moss that muffled the sound of his footsteps. He touched her shoulder, but still she did not turn or speak.

"Sonia, it is sunset!" he hissed, catching at her arm. "Past sunset! The skimmers —"

He broke off as she shivered all over. With astonishment, he saw that her eyes had filled with tears. Then he looked ahead, over her shoulder, and realized why she had stopped and what she was staring at.

Just beyond the two sentinels was a clearing ringed with shadowy fern trunks and open to a brilliant orange sky. Except for the sound of the gurgling water somewhere underground, the clearing was utterly still. In its center was a small round pool, gleaming like a mirror.

Dann's Mirror . . . The words floated into Rye's mind from nowhere. He did not realize he had repeated them aloud until the girl turned to look at him, amazement in her brimming eyes.

"What did you say?" she whispered.

Rye shook his head. He could not explain himself. Pushing past her, he stepped into the clearing and walked the few steps to the pool. He looked down at the glassy surface, and for a brief moment, his reflection floated there, shadowy and mysterious.

Then the water began to ripple. It was as if a pebble had been thrown into the pool or a leaf had fallen. But no stone had been thrown. No leaf marred the dark surface.

The ripples were making a pattern. Rye felt his throat close as he saw a single word appear.

THE FELLAN

R ye swallowed, staring in fear and disbelief at the word rippling in the water. Sonia was behind him. He could hear her rapid breathing and smell the slime that still clung to her clothes.

But the command was for him. He knew it.

All his life, Rye had been taught never to drink wild water. Wild water carried dirt and disease. Only well water and rainwater were safe, and even they were best boiled before drinking.

He remembered the rule and dismissed it. Without hesitation, he slid the bell tree stick into his belt and dropped to his knees beside the pool.

He felt Sonia plucking at his sleeve, heard her whispering to him urgently, warning him of poison, of enchantment, of danger.

He dipped his cupped hands into the pool, bent his head, and drank.

Never had he tasted such water. It was as different from the water of Weld as bread fresh from the oven is different from stale crusts. Cool, sweet, and clear, it slipped down his dry throat like sparkling nectar, bringing with it instant refreshment and a feeling that he was twice as alive as he had been before.

Eagerly he dipped his hands back into the pool and drank again. And again.

It is enough.

Rye looked up, startled, water dribbling down his chin and soaking into his shirt. Behind him, Sonia gave a small, choking cry.

Hooded figures were peeling from the trunks of the giant ferns that surrounded the clearing. They were brown, like the fern stems, and their long robes were dark brown, too, but as they glided toward the pond, their color began to change to green.

Rye could not move. He could not breathe. Sonia was gripping his arm so tightly that it hurt.

Then the figures were all around them. Rye stared wordlessly up at the ring of smooth green faces — ageless faces, with pointed chins, high cheekbones, and brows that slanted over the dark pools of their eyes. They were male and female, both. He could see that, despite the hoods. Some of the faces were slightly smiling. Others were alive with what looked like curiosity. A few were very grave.

These beings could not be barbarians — surely they could not! They looked nothing like the hulking brutes in pictures Rye had seen. They carried no weapons. And they could change color, to hide themselves, like the monstrous lizards. He had never heard that barbarians could do that.

Who were they, then? And why were they standing here, in the open air, unafraid of sunset and the skimmers?

Rye was suddenly seized by the terrible fear that Dirk, and all the other volunteers who had chosen the golden Door, had made a fatal error. What if the Door had delivered them not into the wilds of Dorne but into another land entirely?

Slowly he felt for the stick in his belt. He had tried to move without being seen, but the instant his fingers touched the smooth wood, the figures around the pool murmured and looked down at his hand.

Rye knew he had to face these beings on his feet, or he and Sonia would have no chance at all. Slowly, trying not to make any sudden moves that might seem like a threat, he stood up, drawing Sonia up with him.

One of the females pulled back her hood. Her skin changed again, fading to pale gold, as gleaming red braids of hair tumbled over her shoulders and down her back. Her companions followed her lead. All of them had the same long braids, and all of the braids flamed in the orange light of the sky.

Rye heard Sonia draw a shuddering breath. He gripped his stick. It was not much of a weapon, but it was all he had.

"What place is this, if you please?" he asked, trying with all his might to keep his voice from trembling.

The strange beings looked at one another, then back at him.

"He seeks to deceive us," the tallest of the men muttered. "He knows where he is. His companion said the words 'Fell Zone' more than once."

Rye's stomach fluttered. "I am not trying to deceive you!" he exclaimed. "But I do not understand. If this is the Fell Zone of Dorne, then who are you?"

"Knowledge of us has been lost in the city of Dann, it seems, Kirwan," the woman who had first removed her hood said softly to the tall man.

As he scowled, she turned to Rye. He felt himself caught and held by her amazing eyes, which now looked more green than brown.

"We are the Fellan," she said. "We are the tenants of this place your people call the Fell Zone. We have been expecting you."

Rye gaped at her. Then suddenly his heart leaped, and he felt the blood rush into his face.

"*Expecting* me?" he gasped. "You mean you met my brother Dirk? He told you I might come? Did he leave a message for me?"

He felt a crushing wave of disappointment as the woman looked surprised, and shook her head.

"We know nothing of those who came before you," she murmured.

"They came thundering into our territory like storm clouds and vanished just as quickly," the man called Kirwan said stiffly. "A few reached this place, fell foul of Dann's Mirror, and fled downstream. The bones of the rest lie under the leaves or in the nets of the fell-dragons."

Rye's mind was spinning with disappointment, confusion, and fear. "Then why — how — have you been expecting me?" he stammered.

"We were given three signs by which we would know the one we awaited," the woman answered calmly. "We did not guess that you would be so young or that you would be one among many, but the signs have all been fulfilled."

"What does she mean?" Sonia hissed in Rye's ear. "What signs? Rye — what game have you been playing?"

As the woman's eyes moved from his face to Sonia's, Rye felt a little jolt, as if a thread that had been holding him tightly had suddenly snapped.

Desperately he tried to collect his thoughts. He knew full well that he could not be the person the Fellan had been waiting for. Except for Dirk and the other volunteers from Southwall, no one on this side of the Wall of Weld knew of his existence.

Should he tell the Fellan they were wrong, or say nothing? Which would be safer?

"The first two signs were not perfect, Edelle," Kirwan said.

"Indeed," another man agreed. "And he took up the barbarian weapon to pursue the fell-dragon."

"He used it only to cut a dragon net and save his companion," the woman called Edelle argued. "The iron left him when he needed it no longer. Besides, the test of Dann's Mirror has made the other signs of no importance. The Mirror knew him. He drank not just once but three times. He is the one."

There was a murmur of agreement around the pool. Kirwan hesitated, but at last even he reluctantly nodded.

Edelle stepped out of the circle and moved to Rye's side.

"Say your name, if you please," she murmured.

"R-Rye," Rye stammered, startled into speech. "Rye, third son of Lisbeth and Kaz, brother to Dirk and Sholto."

"Third son," someone in the circle repeated.

Edelle made no sign that she had heard. She opened her hand and showed Rye the object that had been concealed within it.

It was a small brown bag, its neck drawn tightly closed by a long loop of braided red cord. It looked like one of the charms that some old-fashioned citizens of Weld hung over their doors to ward off evil.

"We were given this in trust for you," Edelle said. "It contains nine powers to aid you in your quest. We swore to keep it safe and to give it to you when you came to us. In return, you must swear never to tell a living soul how you came by it. Do you so swear?"

Rye went cold. He was caught in a net from which there was no escape. How dearly did he wish that he had stopped this at the very beginning! Now it was too late. He had blundered upon knowledge of a deadly secret. If he told the truth now, he and Sonia would never be allowed to leave this place.

"Do you so swear?" Edelle repeated.

Rye nodded. "Yes," he croaked. "I swear."

With the air of one conferring a great honor, Edelle slipped the circle of cord over Rye's head. He felt the little bag settle onto his chest, and put up his hand to touch it. The bag was faintly warm, and his fingers tingled as they brushed its velvety surface.

Magic . . . magic that was intended for another.

Rye's stomach churned. It was all he could do to stop himself from tearing the cord from his neck and thrusting the little bag back at Edelle.

"I thank you," he made himself say.

Edelle paused, then leaned closer, pretending to straighten the cord at the back of his neck.

"You must make haste," she breathed close to his ear. "Time is short. It is almost Midsummer Eve."

"Edelle!" Kirwan's voice was sharp.

"So our promise has been fulfilled," Edelle said aloud and stepped back.

The other Fellan seemed to sigh, as if a great weight had been lifted from their shoulders. Then they all pulled their concealing hoods over their heads and began gliding silently back toward the giant ferns. Avoiding Kirwan's accusing eyes, Edelle pulled up her own hood and followed.

"Wait!" Sonia cried. "Do not leave us!"

"Be quiet, Sonia!" Rye muttered furiously, but the girl took no notice.

"If you are on our side, you must show us where to go!" she shouted at the Fellan. "You must help us!"

Edelle stopped, but Kirwan put a warning hand on her arm and looked around, frowning. His face was already shadowy green.

"We are on no *side*," he said. "By ancient treaty, we do not interfere in the wider affairs of Dorne. We took charge of the gift we have passed to you for the sake of an old friendship, but we can do no more." He glanced at Edelle, silent beside him. "Already, perhaps, we have done too much."

He turned away and moved swiftly after the others, drawing Edelle along with him. In moments, they had vanished into the ferns.

Sonia made an impatient sound and threw herself down by the pool. She scooped up a handful of water and carried it to her lips.

The next moment, she was coughing, spluttering, and spitting in disgust.

"Ah, it is foul!" she choked, jumping up and scrubbing her lips with the back of her hand. "Bitter as week-old wine dregs! How could you drink it?"

Rye stared at her, astounded, as she continued to cough and spit. He crouched by the pool himself and took a small, careful sip. The water tasted as sweet and pure as ever.

"I do not understand you," he said, dipping his hand into the pool again. "I have never tasted better."

Sonia fell silent. He took a final drink, stood up, and turned to look at her. She was watching him intently — almost fearfully.

"It is the sign," she said in a low voice. "The final sign that convinced them to give you that charm you wear around your neck. The water in Dann's Mirror is sweet for you, but for no one else."

It was plain to Rye that she was so used to the bland boiled and filtered water of the Keep that wild water was simply too strong for her taste. He could not say so aloud, however. The Fellan might still be close enough to hear. He could not risk talking disdainfully of the "sign" in which they had put so much faith.

"So it seems you are not as ordinary as you pretend," Sonia muttered, glancing at him sideways. "Well, keep your secret, if it is so important to you! But surely you could have tried to make the Fellan help us! As it is, we do not know which way to go from here, or even where to take safe shelter for the night."

"Then we are no worse off than we were before," said Rye.

"Of course we are!" she cried. "Soon it will be dark. We do not dare to move on without a guide, in case we run into a fell-dragon net! And we cannot stay in this clearing, under the sky. You know that! You are the one who is so obsessed with skimmers!"

In sudden dread, Rye looked up. The orange light had faded. The sky above the clearing was gray, and he thought he could see the first glimmer of a star. To his relief, no dark, ragged shapes were flapping overhead.

"The first wave must fly to Weld from another direction," said Sonia. "But who knows when others may come this way?"

Helplessly, Rye looked around the deserted clearing, which was now ringed with shadows. He thought he caught a flicker of movement and froze, staring at the place. The longer he looked, the more convinced he became that one shadow was deeper than the others.

Ask Dann's Mirror. . . .

The whisper was so faint that he was not certain that he had really heard it, yet he seemed to recognize the voice. He blinked, and suddenly the deeper shadow had vanished.

"Thank you, Edelle," he murmured.

"What?" Sonia demanded irritably.

Rye stepped back to the edge of the pool and looked down into the dim water. Had Edelle really meant that he could ask the pool a question, and it would answer him?

He crouched by the pool. His reflection was now just a dark, blurred shape on the glassy surface.

Whatever he asked, he had to ask it quickly. Soon it would be too dark to see.

A dozen questions trembled on his tongue. There were so many things he did not understand. So many things he needed to know.

But one was more important than all the rest. He could not miss this chance to ask it.

"Where is my brother Dirk?" he whispered.

The water began to ripple. Words appeared. Rye strained his eyes to make them out.

In the place of the Enemy.

Rye's heart seemed to leap into his throat.

"Where is the place of the Enemy?" he heard himself ask. "How do I get there?"

The darkening water swirled. New words formed.

The stream will guide you safely through the night. Your goal is the city called Ottan.

UNDER THE STARS

R ye and Sonia followed the stream through the howls and screeches of the Fell Zone night. Leaves rustled, sticks cracked, and hungry eyes glittered in the blackness that fringed their path. But nothing sprang at them out of the blackness, and no nets barred their way.

At first, they had to walk blindly, guided only by the sound of water running beneath the mossy rock on which they trod. Then, just as the moon rose above the trees, the stream reappeared, bubbling from beneath a shelf of rock. After that, it was their constant companion, babbling beside them, winding ahead of them like a rippling ribbon of light.

It was a comfort, but the sense of danger was still very great, and Rye and Sonia walked tensely and in silence, not daring to stop for rest.

The bell tree stick held at the ready, Rye kept

glancing up at the narrow band of sky above his head, checking for signs of skimmers.

There were no skimmers, or none that he could see. But there were stars — countless stars, studding the inky sky. Soon Rye found he was looking up as much in fascination as in fear. Never had he seen stars like these. The pale pinpoints of light that glimmered in the hazy night sky of Weld were nothing compared to this dazzling array of jewels glittering in a deep black sea.

"How beautiful they are!" Sonia whispered beside him. "I had no idea stars could be so beautiful!"

"Nor I," said Rye. "It must be because the sky at home is never as clear as this."

And all at once, the fierce, uncaring brilliance of the stars blurred before his eyes, and he felt a terrible longing to be back beneath a softer sky, among the things he knew, behind the high Wall of Weld.

It is no use thinking of that, he told himself furiously. *There is no going back. And home is no longer home as it was. Is that not why you are here?*

"You deceived the Warden in more ways than one, Rye," Sonia said quietly. "You did not leave Weld to find the source of the skimmers and win the reward, did you? You want only to find your brother! That is why you chose the golden Door. It was the one you thought Dirk must have taken."

Rye did not bother to deny it. Sonia had heard his first question at the pool.

"Dirk is in the place of the Enemy, so as it happens, you have not wasted your time by coming with me," he muttered. "When we reach Oltan, we can go our separate ways. I will find Dirk, to take him home, and you can destroy the Enemy — if you are able."

"There is nothing to say that the Enemy of Oltan is the one who is sending skimmers to Weld!" Sonia snapped, stung by his tone.

"Dirk plainly thinks he is," Rye said stoutly. "I may not have come here hoping to stop the skimmers, but Dirk did! If he is in Oltan, he is not there for nothing, you can depend upon it."

He heard a stealthy stirring in the bushes on the other side of the stream. Realizing that he had slowed, he moved quickly on, deliberately lengthening his stride so that Sonia was forced to fall behind. After that, he glanced at the sky less often, and when he did, he tried not to think of the stars.

He meant to keep up a brisk pace and to stay alert to danger, but as time slipped by, he found it harder and harder. Sonia was so silent that he had to keep looking over his shoulder to make sure she was still following.

We will soon reach the end of the Fell Zone, he told himself, remembering the schoolroom map. And that means we will soon be on the coast — in Oltan. No one will be stirring at this time of night. We will find shelter, and then we can rest.

But the stream wound on and on, the seething blackness beyond its banks never grew still, and the snarls and howls of invisible creatures killing and being killed never became less. And all Rye and Sonia could do was to move forward, driven by fear, keeping on their feet by pure will.

At last, however, there came a time when the ferns ended, the stream banks flattened and widened, and the trees became fewer.

"We are almost there, I think," Rye called over his shoulder.

His voice sounded hoarse. It was hours since he had spoken aloud.

Sonia did not answer. Rye looked back and saw that between the streaks of dirt on the girl's face, her skin was sickly pale. Her eyelids were drooping. She was stumbling as she walked.

He saw that she was exhausted. And only then did he realize how exhausted he was himself.

How long had they been following the stream? He could barely remember the last part of the journey. It was as if he had been walking in a dream.

"Just a little farther," he called to Sonia and waited for her to catch up to him. She blinked, swaying like someone just woken from sleep.

Fearing she would fall, Rye took her arm. She made no protest. Cautiously they crept together out of the trees and stopped, staring.

A humpbacked stone bridge spanned the stream ahead. A bare dirt track trailed away on either side of the bridge, disappearing into the shadowy distance.

Beyond the track, there was open land divided here and there by straggling fences and dotted with small groups of trees. The land reared up into hills and sank into shallow valleys in a way Rye found disturbing and unnatural. Above the whole arched a vast, star-studded sky.

There were no houses to be seen. No shops or halls. No buildings at all. The only signs of human life were the fences, the bridge, and the road.

"This cannot be," Rye said slowly.

Sonia's eyes were huge in her pale, drawn face. Abruptly she pulled away from Rye, crouched beside the stream, and began splashing herself with water. When she stood up, her face, arms, and clothes were wet, and she no longer looked half-asleep.

"Where is the city?" she demanded. "And where is the sea? Surely we should be able to see it from here. The maps in all my books —"

"Mine, too," said Rye.

A clammy coldness was creeping over him. He did not know what to believe. Either the Fellan had lied, and this land was not Dorne at all, or the map he had seen every day of his school life, the map upon which he had depended, was terribly, bizarrely, wrong.

It took only a moment for him to decide that he would rather trust the Fellan than the map. Why, he had not even known the Fellan existed until he had seen them with his own eyes! He had always been taught that the Fell Zone was nothing but a safety barrier for Weld — a forbidden belt of land dreaded by the barbarians and filled with monsters.

If he had not known about the people of the Fell Zone, what else did he not know about the land beyond the Wall of Weld?

He felt suddenly overwhelmed by exhaustion. It was all he could do to stop himself sinking to the ground. If he had been alone, perhaps he would have done it. But Sonia was with him, and pride kept him upright. He was determined not to show weakness before her again.

Deciding to follow her example, he bent to the stream and splashed his face vigorously. The shock of the cold water made him gasp, but when he stood up, his head felt clearer.

"Still no skimmers," Sonia said, scanning the sky. "Well, that seems to settle one question, at least. The skimmers do not menace Dorne as a whole. Only Weld."

"Dirk was always sure of it," said Rye. It was a relief to speak his brother's name. It made him feel stronger, steadier on his feet.

"If Dirk could find Oltan, we can find it, too," he went on. "It cannot be far away. And surely there will be signposts, now we are out of the Fell Zone."

They moved farther along the stream, then left it and climbed up to the little stone bridge.

Tired as he was, Rye had been quite looking forward to standing on the bridge. The only bridges in Weld were those that spanned the brick trench, and these were forbidden to all but Wall workers. His pleasure was spoiled when he saw that one of the bridge's inner walls was defaced by a string of roughly painted words.

THE GIFTING MUST CEASE!

"How could anyone — even barbarians — splash paint on fine stone like that?" Rye muttered.

"This reminds me of the scribbles on the skimmer notices at home," said Sonia, gazing at the painted words with interest. "Oh, how those scribbles enraged the Warden!"

She smirked, clearly enjoying the memory. "Whenever the soldiers brought a damaged sign back to the Keep, he — the Warden — would lose his temper. Then he would order the notice to be burned. Burned in the courtyard, too, so everyone could see."

Rye's frown deepened. "This is not at all the same! *The gifting must cease* — it is nonsensical! To give a gift is a good thing, not a bad one."

Sonia shrugged. "We do not know how things are done out here. For all we know, there may be a very good reason for — Oh!"

The sudden exclamation made Rye spin around in fright, but Sonia was looking excited rather than alarmed. She was pointing along the road.

"There!" she whispered. "Look there, Rye! There, in the field, just beyond that grove of trees! A house!"

Rye narrowed his eyes, peering down through the shadows. Slowly he made out a small, humped shape not too far from the road's edge.

"If we knock, the owners will surely give us beds for the night," Sonia said happily. "And in the morning, we can ask them the way to Oltan!"

Rye shook his head, marveling that she could allow her hopes to deceive her eyes and her mind so thoroughly.

"That is not a house, Sonia," he said. "It is far too small and low, even for barbarians. At best, it is a shed for animals."

"Oh," the girl said in a small voice and gave a forced little laugh.

"But it is very lucky you spied it," Rye hurried on, seeing that she felt foolish as well as disappointed, and wanting to make her feel better. "It is shelter — and better shelter for us than a house. In the land of the barbarians, it would be unwise to trust in the kindness of strangers."

"Perhaps," Sonia murmured, but looked a little happier.

They left the bridge and walked together down the road toward the rounded building. The field in which it stood had once been separated from the road by a wooden fence, but now a whole section of the fence lay flat and trampled on the ground.

In Weld, it would have been unforgivable to enter another citizen's property with no intention of asking permission. But Rye felt only a tiny twinge of unease as he stepped across the ruined fence and made for the shelter.

Tired to his bones, all he could think of was his need for rest, and it seemed that Sonia felt the same, for she followed him into the field without hesitation.

As they approached the shelter, Rye smelled the faint, familiar scent of goat droppings. There was another odor, too, stronger and sharper, which he did not recognize.

"This *is* a place for animals." Sonia wrinkled her nose. "I hope there are none in there now."

"If there were, they would be calling to us by this time," said Rye. "Come on!"

With the girl trailing after him, he prowled around the shelter, looking for the entrance.

He found himself surprised and impressed. The shed was very sturdy — not at all like the ramshackle building he would have expected barbarians to throw together. It was neatly built of stone, like the bridge. The low roof was flat, made of hard gray sheets that shone like some sort of metal. At a distance, the roof had looked rounded because of the rocks that had been piled on top of the metal sheets to hold them in place.

"Perhaps they have skimmers here, after all," he muttered. He glanced quickly at the sky but could see no movement there.

On the side of the shed farthest from the road, he found a strong wooden door bound with metal bands and fastened with an iron rod. Rye pulled the rod back, opened the door a little, and peered cautiously into the shelter. It was very dark and smelled strongly of goat, but as far as he could see, it was completely empty except for the layer of straw that covered the floor.

He pulled the door wider and noted a second metal bar fixed to the inside frame. "You can bar this door from the inside as well as from the outside," he said in surprise. "It looks as if people do use this shelter sometimes. I wonder why —?"

"Rye . . ." Sonia said in a tense, level voice more chilling than any scream. "Behind you!"

Rye spun around. And there, lumbering toward them from the shadows of the nearby knot of trees, was a shaggy beast with tiny, hungry red eyes and a single white horn that jutted up from its muzzle like a curved sword.

It was big — bigger than a goat by far — bigger than six goats put together! As Rye stared, aghast, the creature grunted and pawed the ground. Its slavering jaws parted, showing blunt, yellow teeth in what looked horribly like a mocking grin. Then it lowered its head and charged.

NINE POWERS

There was only one thing to do. Rye and Sonia flung themselves into the darkness of the hut, dragging the door shut behind them.

Crawling on his hands and knees, Rye fumbled for the iron bar, found it, and thrust it across the door with all his strength. A split second later, there was a thunderous crash as the charging beast slammed into the wood. The door shuddered, but held.

The beast outside bellowed its rage. Again it attacked the door. And again.

"We are safe here," Rye shouted, reaching out for Sonia in the dark. "We are safe. The door must have been made for this. It will not break."

"No," she agreed through chattering teeth. "It will not break."

But as crash after frightful crash shook the door, it seemed impossible that it would not give way. Rye and Sonia clung together, listening to the squealing bellows of the beast. Both of them kept repeating that the door was strong, that the door would hold. Both of them secretly waited in terror for the sounds of splintering wood and tearing metal that would signal the end.

And then, suddenly, the attacks on the door ceased. Rye held his breath, his ears ringing in the silence. Then, through the walls, he heard scrabbling, scraping, and scuffling as the beast went slowly around the hut, nudging at the stones, looking for a weakness.

It circled the shelter once, twice, snorting and grumbling. Then, at last, he could hear it no more.

"It has gone," Sonia breathed. With a sigh of relief, she slumped against the wall.

"It may not have gone far," Rye said grimly. "We can only hope it finds other prey soon so it will forget about us. I do not like the idea of being trapped for more than a night in this smelly goat house."

"Do not call it names," Sonia joked feebly. "This shelter saved us. Finding it was a great piece of good fortune."

It seemed more like a great piece of *bad* fortune to Rye. He was fairly sure that the horned beast kept watch on the hut because the hut often housed the goats it liked to eat. If he and Sonia had never come near the place, they might never have been attacked.

"It was the Fellan charm that brought us luck, no doubt," Sonia went on. "The nine-powers charm."

Rye had forgotten all about the charm. He put his hand up to the little bag hanging around his neck. His fingers tingled, and he snatched them away again.

It suddenly came to him that perhaps the charm had brought him bad luck because it was not rightfully his.

He seemed to see his mother and Dirk nodding seriously. He seemed to hear Sholto scoffing at the very idea.

He lifted the cord over his head. He slipped his thumb and two first fingers into the little bag and began to feel the objects jumbled inside it.

Something soft — a feather, he was sure of it. Something twisted in paper, like a pill or a sweet. Something hard and knobbly . . .

And suddenly, the tiny bag lit up like a lantern.

Rye yelled in shock and pulled his fingers out of the bag. The light went out.

"Oh!" Sonia cried in excitement. "A light! A magic light! Make it shine again!"

Not sure he was doing the wisest thing but far too curious not to try, Rye pushed his fingers back into the bag. Cautiously he groped for the knobbly object he had been holding when the light went on.

The moment he found it and grasped it between finger and thumb, the light appeared once more. Carefully, Rye drew the object out and held it up.

It was a crystal, no bigger than a honey bush berry, but shining more brightly than a lantern a hundred times its size. Now that it was out of the bag, the light that beamed from it was strong enough to flood every corner of the hut.

It was strong enough to show Rye that he had been right. He and Sonia were not the first people to have taken shelter in the goat house.

Words had been scratched on many of the stones of the back wall. The scratches were new, sharp and clear, and every message was the same.

LET ME LIVE! LET OLT DIE!
O, SAVE US FROM MIDSUMMER EVE!

"Wonderful!" Rye heard Sonia sigh. He looked around and saw that she was gazing at the shining crystal in awe.

"Is it hot, Rye?" she asked eagerly.

Rye shook his head. He did not know what to think or how to feel. He could not share Sonia's uncomplicated delight. The crystal *was* wonderful, but it was frightening, too. No thing so small should be so powerful. No ordinary boy of Weld should own it.

He looked down at the little bag.

Nine powers, the Fellan Edelle had said. *Nine powers to aid you in your quest.*

All the guilt that had plagued Rye in the pool clearing came rushing back. He glanced again at the despairing words scratched on the back wall of the shed. Sonia had not noticed them, and he was glad of it. He wished he had never seen them himself.

Something was going to happen on Midsummer Eve. Something terrible, of which the barbarians themselves were afraid.

Edelle had known of it. That was why she had whispered to him, urging him to make haste.

The light crystal and whatever other wonders the little bag contained had been intended for someone who was going to try to stop the dread happening.

And here they were with him.

"I should not have taken this," he muttered, gingerly prodding the bag with a fingertip. "I might just as well have stolen it."

"What in Weld do you mean?" Sonia exclaimed. "The Fellan wanted you to have it."

"They were wrong." Rye shook his head. "I cannot keep it. It is too important. I must return it, and explain —"

"*Return* it?" Sonia exploded, sitting bolt upright. "Go back into the Fell Zone, when it has just taken us so long to get out?"

Rye set his lips stubbornly. He told himself that he had to do what was right, whatever the cost.

Sonia was eyeing him as if he had taken leave of his senses. "Rye, do you want to find your brother or not?" she demanded.

Rye glared at her.

"Then behave as if you do!" she snapped. "Thank

the Wall that magic has fallen into your hands, because in the days to come, you will certainly need it!"

It was like being dashed with icy water, full in the face. Shocked and sobered, Rye stared at the blazing crystal in his hand. He looked down at the little bag on his lap and thought of all the other amazing powers it might contain. Things, perhaps, that would help him find Dirk — save Dirk, who was in danger.

Was the unknown barbarian who had scratched the pleas on the back wall of the shelter more important to him than Dirk? Was his own honor more important to him than Dirk?

Rye knew that they were not. A cold, hard determination slid like a shield between his conscience and his need.

"Hold this," he said, thrusting the crystal at Sonia and picking up the little bag. "I will see what else is here."

But the instant the crystal left his fingers, its light went out. It shone again only when Rye took it back. In the end, he was forced to keep hold of it in one hand and search the bag with the other.

He began with his heart beating fast, but gradually puzzled disappointment took the place of excitement. The things remaining in the bag seemed very ordinary compared to the light crystal. He had expected wonders, but nothing astonishing happened as he held each object up before placing it on his knee with the others.

When he had finished, he and Sonia gazed at the motley collection in silence.

A red feather, slightly ragged around the edges. A shabby ring made of tightly braided gray threads. A tiny gold key. A little brown ball that looked like some sort of nut. A curiously patterned snail shell. The twist of waxed paper, which by its smell seemed to contain a stale honey sweet.

To Rye, the items looked like nothing more than the sorts of interesting but rubbishy treasures he used to collect in his pockets when he was young.

Telling himself that this could not be true, that any objects packed in a bag with the light crystal could not possibly be ordinary, he picked up the ring and slid it on. He waited self-consciously for something to happen — for Sonia to cry out that he had become invisible, for example, or for a feeling of superhuman strength to flow through him.

But he could feel no difference in himself, and the ring did nothing at all.

"All these things are magic," Sonia murmured beside him. "I am sure they are. But what do they do?"

"We may never know, if they only show their powers when they are needed, as the light crystal did," Rye said lightly, trying to hide how crestfallen he felt. "That is the trouble with stolen magic, I daresay."

Sonia put her head on one side.

"You have found only seven things so far,

counting the crystal," she pointed out. "Did the Fellan not tell you there were nine powers in all?"

Rye put his fingers back into the little bag and felt something small and flat wedged into one of the corners. He eased it out carefully.

It was a transparent disc, thin as paper and not much bigger than his thumbnail. As he held it up, it shone blue and green in the light.

"What is it?" Sonia leaned closer.

Rye shrugged uneasily. The strange disc had done nothing, but as he looked at its glimmering surface, a deep trembling began in the pit of his stomach.

"That still only makes eight," Sonia said. "There must be something else. Look again!"

Rye shook his head. "There is nothing else."

He pushed the disc back into the bag and instantly felt better.

"We will think about it again in the morning," he said, scooping up all the other objects on his knee and returning them to the bag, too. "We should try to get some sleep. I only wish I still had that box of supplies I was given. I am starving."

Sonia grinned. "I can do better than stale volunteers' food."

She untied the bag she carried at her waist and rummaged inside it.

"Here!" she said, pulling out some little bundles wrapped in red cloth. "I have dried bell tree fruit and hoji nuts. I have cheese and honey. I have rice pastries, rolls, and sweet cakes. And a flask of amber tea."

She met Rye's startled gaze defiantly. "Yes, I stole them from the Keep kitchens. But will you reject them for that?"

Rye laughed and shook his head.

Gratefully they ate and drank. Then, yawning, they settled themselves for sleep. Rye put the light crystal back into the little drawstring bag, and once again, they were plunged into darkness.

Rye lay back on the straw, finding that despite everything he felt strangely content. His stomach was full. There was silence outside. Cool air blew softly through the tiny gaps between the stones of the walls.

"Ah," he heard Sonia sigh. "How good it is to feel fresh night air! In Weld now, we would be sweltering in our beds."

Sweltering and listening in dread to the skimmers, Rye added silently. He thought of his mother in the Keep — sad and alone, but safe at least.

"Yet here it is warm enough to be comfortable but cool enough to sleep," Sonia was going on drowsily. "Who would guess it was almost Midsummer Eve?"

Rye stared up into darkness. Words scratched on stone seemed to dance in front of his stinging eyes.

LET ME LIVE! LET OLT DIE!
O, SAVE US FROM MIDSUMMER EVE!

THE KINDNESS
OF STRANGERS

Rye slept heavily on his bed of straw. His sleep was filled with dreams of raging bonfires, of dark stone passages, of chains, weeping, and blood. And threading through the dreams like a repeating pattern were images of Dirk, face blackened and fists clenched, repeating over and over again: "Make haste! Time is short. It is almost Midsummer Eve."

Rye woke with a start, a beam of sunlight shining straight into his eyes through a split in the roof. He sat up, confused and panic-stricken. How long had he slept? How much precious time had been lost?

Calling urgently to Sonia, he grabbed the bell tree stick and crawled to the door. His legs and back were aching. His skin itched, and his clothes were stiff with dried mud and slime. Feverishly he unbarred the door and pushed out into the light.

127

He staggered to his feet and took a few stumbling steps forward, his heart still pounding with the panic he had felt on waking. He stared dazedly over bumpy sunlit fields and distant hills, his eyes watering.

Everything looked shockingly bright. The sky above him was a great bowl of cloudless blue — dazzling and unnatural. Behind him, he heard Sonia calling sleepily from the shelter.

Then he heard another sound — a low, menacing sound. And it, too, was coming from somewhere behind him.

His heart seemed to stop. Slowly he looked back.

And there, looming from the side of the shelter, lumbering around the corner to hulk between Rye and the open doorway, was the horned beast.

The beast looked even more fearful in daylight. Its shaggy coat was matted with mud, burrs, and the dried blood of its kills. Its tiny eyes flamed with the hunger of its long hours of waiting. The single yellow-white horn, sharp as a blade, gleamed in the sun as the creature pawed the ground, its foaming jaws stretched into that hideous, grinning, blunt-toothed snarl.

Time seemed to stand still. Thoughts flew and tumbled over one another in Rye's mind, flashing choices at him like a handful of playing cards thrown high into the air.

He could try to dodge around the shelter and get up onto the roof, but the beast was too close. It would be upon him before he could even begin to climb. If he ran toward the road, the creature would certainly catch him before he even reached the flattened fence. If he turned and made for the open fields, he might last a little longer, but the result would be the same.

The fact was, the beast would easily catch him whichever way he ran. He had seen its speed. But run he must, as fast as he could, and not just to try to save himself.

Sonia was in the shelter. At the very least, he had to lead the beast as far away from her as he could, so she had the chance to shut and bar the door.

Rye glanced to his left, to the grove of trees. There was a low-branching tree at the edge nearest the road. He knew it was his best chance.

The beast lowered its head and charged.

Rye yelled, threw the stick wildly, and ran.

Out of the corner of his eye, he saw the beast wheel and come thundering after him. He could hear the creature's grunting bellows and the pounding of its hooves already drawing closer, closer to his heels. The grove of trees seemed very far away.

Run faster, he urged himself in terror. *Faster!*

And then, suddenly, the low-branched tree was right in front of him. Suddenly he was flinging himself up onto the lowest branch, seizing a higher one with sweating, trembling hands, and climbing up, up. . . .

How have I done this? he thought in confusion as he climbed. How did I outrun it?

The tree shook as the beast battered its trunk,

butting and tearing at it in fury. Rye wrapped his arms and legs around the branch he clung to, screwing his eyes shut, pressing his cheek against the rough bark.

Then there was a thud and a piercing squeal.

Rye opened his eyes and looked down.

The horned beast was lying at the foot of the tree. A metal spike was sticking out of its side. Its body jerked once, and was still.

"Got it!" a voice roared from the direction of the road.

Rye peered around the branch and blinked into the sun. A dark, chunky, child-sized figure in a green cap was standing just inside the flattened section of fence. The figure was lowering a glinting metal triangle that was plainly some sort of barbarian bow.

Behind the figure, pulled up in the middle of the road, was a bright green horse-drawn cart loaded with enormous bleating goats. Fixed to the cart's side was a bold white sign.

FITZFEE GOAT FARM
FINE MILK, CHEESE & BUTTER

* HOME DELIVERIES
* FRIENDLY SERVICE
* BEST RATES

Another figure, even smaller than the first and wearing a bunchy striped skirt, sat on the driver's seat of the cart, punching the air with one hand and holding the horse's reins with the other.

"Good shot, Dadda!" the figure in the cart cried, and at the same moment, Rye realized with a shock that the person at the fence was not a child at all but a very short man.

"Ho there!" the short man called, waving to Rye. "You can come down now!" He slung the weapon over his shoulder and began striding toward the tree.

Rye clung to his branch, staring in disbelief. Who were these people, who looked like sturdy children but carried weapons strong enough to slay monsters? And how rich, or how mad, must they be, to use a *horse* to draw their cart, while their giant goats rode?

"Rye!" The bell tree stick clutched in her hand, Sonia ran into Rye's view and came to a skidding halt below him. She looked up, laughing with relief. "Rye, come down! The beast is dead!"

"Dead as a doorknob," the short man agreed, joining her under the tree and nudging the fallen beast with the toe of his boot.

"How can we ever thank you, sir?" cried Sonia. And to Rye's enormous surprise, she dropped a graceful curtsy, which looked very odd indeed in comparison with the mud-smeared rags she wore.

"Ah, say nothing of it!" the little man said, pulling off his green knitted cap and bowing magnificently.

"Magnus FitzFee at your service. Always glad to help a stranger in a fix. And I hate bloodhogs anyhow."

Casually placing his foot on the dead beast's shaggy side to brace himself, he began heaving at the spike jutting from the body.

"We come along, and there's the boy running like a streak of lightning with the bloodhog after him, see," he grunted, pulling at the spike with all his might. "And I say to Popsy, 'Bless my heart,' I say, 'look at that! Did you ever see a fellow run that fast, even with a bloodhog after him?' And Popsy, she says she never has."

With a final, determined heave, he pulled the spike free. Its wicked barb and the lower half of its shaft were thick with dark blood. He crouched to wipe it on the grass.

"So then I say, 'Well, he's got to the tree, but that won't do him much good if we don't give him a hand, will it? Bloodhogs never give up, Popsy, as you know,' I say. 'That mean old specimen will have that tree down in the end. And then that champion young fleet-of-foot will be minced meat in two minutes flat.'"

Sonia smiled and nodded. High in his tree, Rye shuddered.

Having cleaned the spike to his satisfaction, Magnus FitzFee stood up.

"And Popsy says I'm dead right," he went on, stowing the spike in a leather pouch he carried on his back. "So I stop the cart, and get my old crossbow out from under the seat, and do the business. Nothing to it!"

He glanced up at Rye, clearly wondering why he was still in the tree.

"You all right up there?" he called politely.

"Yes, Rye, come *down!*" Sonia laughed.

It is all very well for her, Rye thought resentfully. He wanted very much to climb down. He had been trying to make himself begin for many long minutes. The trouble was, his limbs seemed to have frozen. Every time he looked down, his head swam. Never in his life had he been so high above the ground without a safety harness.

I got up here without a harness, he told himself. *So I can get down.*

He managed it at last, though his legs felt like water and his arms almost as bad. Magnus FitzFee watched the beginning of the ungainly descent, then discreetly turned his back to wave to his daughter on the cart.

"So you're more of a runner than a climber, friend," he said when he heard Rye sighing with relief as he finally reached the ground. "I'm the other way around, myself. Not built for running, but I can climb like a clink."

"What is a clink?" Sonia asked without thinking.

FitzFee spun around. He gaped at Rye, then turned his startled gaze on Sonia. His eyes were blue as chips of sky in his brown face.

"And where would you two be from, that you don't know what a clink is?" he demanded. "Why, there'd not be a house around here that doesn't have a clink or two in the roof!"

There was a heavy silence. Rye saw Sonia's face flush as red as her cap, and could feel the heat rising in his own cheeks and neck.

"We — we are not from around here," he said awkwardly.

"No," murmured Magnus FitzFee, looking keenly from one to the other. "No, I see you aren't. I can't think why I didn't realize it before. That run . . ." He grimaced. "The bloodhog distracted me, I daresay. Well, well."

"Dadda!" called the girl in the cart. "Dadda, come *on*!"

"One minute, Popsy!" FitzFee shouted over his shoulder. "Don't you move, now!"

Rye glared at Sonia. She shrugged uncomfortably. They both made their faces expressionless as FitzFee turned back to them.

"Where are the rest of you?" he asked abruptly. "What are you doing here on your own?"

"We — got lost," Sonia said.

"Lost?" FitzFee frowned and rubbed his mouth with the back of his hand. "Lost . . ."

Again he looked over his shoulder, but this time, he seemed to be gazing past the road, to the tall trees of the Fell Zone. Quickly, almost furtively, he crossed his stubby fingers, and then his wrists.

Rye's stomach lurched. FitzFee had guessed where they had come from! Did that mean he had stumbled across other Weld volunteers who had managed to escape the Fell Zone? It was quite possible, if he lived around here.

Sonia was frowning and gnawing her lip, her eyes fixed on the crossbow slung over the little man's shoulder. Rye knew she was bitterly regretting the slip that had raised FitzFee's suspicions. She feared that now they were in terrible danger.

Rye feared it, too. FitzFee had saved their lives, certainly. But that was before he began to suspect who they were. However friendly he seemed, he was still a barbarian — and the barbarians, one and all, were the savage enemies of Weld.

Somehow they had to convince FitzFee that his suspicions were wrong. They had to turn his thoughts away from the Fell Zone and the walled city hidden in its center.

I will say we are from another island, Rye thought feverishly. I will say our boat was wrecked on the shore of Dorne and that we have been wandering. . . .

"Master FitzFee, we came here —" he began.

"Don't say any more, friend," FitzFee said gruffly, without turning his head. "I don't want to know another thing about you, and what I do know I'm going to forget from now. These are dangerous times, and I've got my family to consider."

He looked back at Rye and Sonia again. His face

135

was very serious, but his eyes had softened with what looked curiously like respectful pity. He thrust his cap at Rye.

"Put this on," he ordered. "You can keep it — I've got plenty more. And let's say no more about this business. As far as I'm concerned, you're just a couple of ordinary, lost young travelers, see? How would a humble goat farmer know any different? You understand me?"

Speechless, they nodded.

"Very good!" FitzFee waited till Rye had put on the knitted cap and pulled it right down over his ears. Then he straightened his shoulders, thrust his hands into his pockets, and gazed up at the dazzling sky.

"Lovely morning, isn't it?" he remarked, in quite a different tone. "So! What will you do now, young travelers? Can a humble goat farmer do anything more to help you?"

Rye took a chance. "You can help us to find our way home," he said carefully. "Home . . . to Oltan."

THE ROAD TO OLTAN

B less my heart!" FitzFee gasped, quickly crossing his fingers and wrists again. *"Oltan?* Just before Midsummer Eve? Have you lost your senses? You, of all people, shouldn't be —"

He suddenly broke off and wiped his mouth with the back of his hand as if to rub out the words he had been about to say. No doubt, Rye thought, he had remembered that he was supposed to be a simple goat farmer helping two lost strangers he knew nothing about.

"Surely you will not refuse to show us our way home?" Sonia urged, keeping up the story they all knew to be a lie.

FitzFee looked left and right, plainly not knowing what to do. Then, abruptly, he gave in.

"The turnoff to Oltan's not too far ahead," he mumbled, his lips barely moving. "There's a signpost —

you can't miss it. You just stay on that road, and in the end, you'll get to Oltan. When you get to Fleet — it's just beyond those hills you can see on the horizon — you'll know you're about halfway."

Rye stared in dismay at the distant hills. How long would it take to walk that far?

"Oh, dear," groaned Sonia. Ruefully she looked down at her slippers, which were already worn almost to rags.

FitzFee heaved a gusty sigh.

"As it happens, Popsy and I are going to Fleet," he said reluctantly. "We can take you that far if . . . if you're sure —"

"We are!" Rye exclaimed in heartfelt relief. "Thank you, Master FitzFee."

"Say nothing of it," the little man muttered, looking far from happy. "Just you keep your heads down, and when we get to Fleet, remember who you are."

"Lost young travelers," said Sonia obediently.

"Quite!" FitzFee nodded. "The Fleet people don't want trouble any more than I do. Especially now, when they're —"

Again he broke off, clearing his throat, and plainly thinking better of what he had been about to say.

It sounded as if the people of Fleet had a secret, too. Rye wondered what it could be, and whether it had anything to do with Midsummer Eve.

But FitzFee had already begun trudging toward the road. He was making it very clear that as far as he was concerned, the subject was closed.

✳

Very soon afterward, Rye and Sonia were jolting along in the green cart, being nuzzled enthusiastically by six large and curious goats.

Popsy had been thrilled to hear that her father was going to give the lost travelers a ride to Fleet. As Rye climbed into the cart, she gazed at him with embarrassing admiration.

"You run very fast," she lisped. "Fast and faster! Are you a magic man?"

"Don't talk foolish, Popsy!" her father ordered, shaking the horse's reins, and the little girl giggled and hid her face in her hands.

"But you did run very fast, Rye," Sonia whispered when they were well under way and Popsy had begun pestering her father with questions about how long it would take to get to Fleet. "I saw you, from the goat house. You suddenly — just took off! It was incredible!"

"It is incredible how fast you can run when a bloodhog is trying to turn you into minced meat," muttered Rye. But uneasily he remembered how startled he had been to find the low-branched tree looming in front of him, when just an instant before it had seemed so far away.

I am not a bad runner, he thought. But I am not

that good. I cannot beat Dirk. So how in Weld did I outrun the bloodhog?

And then, by chance, the cart hit a hole in the road, and he found himself thrown off balance, recovering, and staring at his hands clutching the cart's side.

Only then did he realize that he was still wearing the ring he had put on the night before. He had not returned it to the little bag with the other things. He had forgotten all about it.

He stared down at it. It looked so ordinary. Gray threads, woven into a simple circle. And yet . . .

"The ring!" he breathed. "The ring helped me run!"

Sonia turned to look at him, her eyes wide.

"That is its power!" Rye hissed. "Speed! Speed when you need it! But how could I have known?"

"Look in the bag again!" Sonia urged. "Perhaps this morning you can find the ninth power, and we can work out what the other things do as well!"

But though he was longing to do as she asked, Rye did not dare risk it. Not in the open air, in a breezy, jolting cart. The things in the bag were so small. It would be all too easy for one of them to slip through his fingers or blow away.

"When we get to Fleet," he said. "When we are inside and on our own."

He scratched his head through the knitted cap.

He was not used to wearing anything on his head, and the cap felt prickly.

"I do not know why FitzFee made me wear this," he muttered. "It is not much of a disguise, and it is very uncomfortable."

"Oh, you will soon get used to it," said Sonia, pulling her own cap down almost to her eyebrows and making it look worse than ever. "I did. I found I had to wear one when I started moving through the Keep chimneys, or my hair got full of soot."

At that moment, the horse slowed and the cart began to turn to the right. Craning his neck around the goats, Rye saw a signpost — the first he had seen since leaving Weld.

"Look, Dadda!" cried Popsy in great excitement. "A bad person drawed on the sign! They crossed out Oltan and put another name instead!"

FitzFee mumbled and clicked his tongue to the horse to make it go faster. His neck and back had stiffened. Rye could feel his tension as if it were his own. He was certain that the little man wanted to turn his head and see how his passengers were reacting to the changed sign but did not dare to do so.

"*Ne-rra*," Popsy read slowly. "What's Nerra?"

"Oh, that's nothing. It's just what Oltan used to be called before Chieftain Olt changed its name to be like his."

FitzFee was trying to sound careless, but his voice was shaking a little. It could have been because of the jolting of the cart, but Rye did not think so, and as he met Sonia's eyes he realized that she did not think so either. They could both hear that FitzFee was afraid.

Olt, Rye thought, his spine tingling, a picture of words scratched on a stone wall filling his mind.

"Didn't people like Chieftain Olt changing the name?" Popsy asked. "Is that why —?"

"Don't you worry your head about it, Popsy," FitzFee cut in sharply. "It's nothing to do with you. It happened a long time ago, when you were a baby."

"I'm not a baby now," the girl said. "Tigg is a baby, but I'm five!"

"So you are," said FitzFee, very seriously. "You're a big girl. Big enough and clever enough to promise never to say that old Nerra name to anyone, hear me? You just forget it. Chieftain Olt has forbidden it."

"Is it a bad name?" Popsy asked with interest. "Is it like El —?"

But FitzFee at once began to sing loudly, shaking the reins and stamping his feet in time with the tune, until the little girl could not resist joining in.

"You were right, Rye!" Sonia whispered excitedly. "This tyrant — Chieftain Olt — must be our Enemy.

He has conquered his own people, and now he is using skimmers to make war on Weld!"

Rye did not answer. He was grappling with a new, chilling idea.

"Rye?" Sonia nudged him impatiently.

Rye wet his lips. "Sonia, something is going to happen on Midsummer Eve," he said, keeping his voice very low. "Something terrible."

"Why do you say that?" asked Sonia. "Just because FitzFee —?"

"No. The Fellan Edelle whispered something about Midsummer Eve to me as well, when she gave me this." Rye touched the little bag hanging around his neck. "And there was something else."

Sonia listened closely as he told her of the words he had seen on the back wall of the goat shelter, but when he had finished, she merely shrugged.

"So? Whatever the danger is, it is surely between Olt and his people. It has nothing to do with us."

"It might have everything to do with us," Rye said grimly. "What if the person who wrote those words was not a barbarian at all? What if he was a Weld volunteer, who took shelter in the goat shed, just as we did?"

"But you said the writing looked new!" Sonia objected. "And you are the first volunteer to leave Weld for —"

"This volunteer might have been *returning* to

Weld — or trying to," said Rye. "He might have been trying to escape!"

"Running away?" Sonia made a wry face. "I would not have thought that any of the splendid heroes who chose the golden Door had enough sense for that!"

"Do not joke, Sonia," Rye begged. "Listen to me! FitzFee knew who we were. He was afraid to talk about it, but he knew. I have been thinking that he cannot be the only one to be aware that Weld volunteers are coming here. And if the ordinary people are aware . . ."

"Sooner or later, Olt would hear of it, too," Sonia said slowly, following his reasoning at last. "Then he would try to find the spies out. Search for them. Capture them." Her face was very serious now.

Rye nodded, swallowing hard. "Midsummer Eve is a time to celebrate. And . . . what better way for a tyrant to celebrate than to publicly execute captured enemy spies? How better to show his power?"

Sonia frowned. "You are jumping to conclusions. No one has said anything about executions on Midsummer Eve. You cannot know —"

"I can!" Rye hesitated, fearing she would jeer at him, then forced himself to go on. "I dreamed of it, Sonia! I saw blood, masses of blood. I saw chains, and fires. I saw Dirk, begging me to make haste."

Sonia stared at him, very startled.

"You dreamed of it," she repeated in a flat voice.

"Yes!" Rye said defiantly. "And my dreams are true, I know it! Believe me or not, as you like."

Sonia fell silent, biting her lip.

The cart rattled and jolted. FitzFee was still singing, Popsy piping along with him. The goats grew bored, settled down on the straw that cushioned the floor of the cart, and sat lazily chewing their cud. Rye stared out at the rich green and gold countryside slipping by.

Every now and then he saw people working in the fields. None of them looked like Magnus FitzFee. They were more like the barbarians Rye had seen pictured in books — tall, broad-shouldered, and roughly dressed. The younger ones, male and female, all had bandaged heads and arms or were limping, as if they had been fighting. They did not look particularly savage, however, and many of them paused, straightened their backs and waved as the cart went by.

"Midsummer Eve is tomorrow," Sonia said at last. "Still, half a day and a night should give us plenty of time to get to Oltan, overthrow a tyrant, and save his prisoners — do you not agree?" The corner of her mouth twitched.

"Oh, certainly," Rye said, trying to match her tone. He knew this was Sonia's way of saying she was with him, whether he was right or wrong about Olt's plans for Midsummer Eve.

They passed a small village, where ducks of many colors paddled in a pond, lines of washing flapped in the sun, and little children ran about barefoot. Most of the older people were occupied in making a great pile of sticks and logs in the center of the square. The people all looked healthy and well fed, but there was not a smile among them.

"Midsummer Eve!" cried Popsy, breaking off her song and clapping her hands at the sight of the growing bonfire heap. "One more sleep!"

"That's right," said her father tightly. And this time he could not resist throwing a dark look over his shoulder at his silent passengers.

"Best you get some rest while you can, young travelers," he said gruffly. "There's a way to go yet."

He lowered his voice so Popsy would not hear him. "And when we get to Fleet, just keep your mouths shut. Ask no questions and you'll be told no lies, as my old gran used to say. Understand?"

He scowled until they had both nodded. Then he turned back to face the front, clicked to the horse, and drove on.

FLEET

Fleet was a surprise. At FitzFee's warning call, Rye woke from an uneasy doze to see before him a graceful township that seemed to be filled with flowers. It was not at all the sort of place he had expected to find in the land of the barbarians.

"How beautiful!" Sonia was exclaiming. "And, oh! Look at the *horses*!"

Rich fields edged with white painted fences surrounded the town. And in the fields were horses — wonderful horses, brown, white, black, and dappled gray, with proud, arching necks and fine, long legs. The younger ones galloped along the side fences with the cart. The older ones just stood watching the newcomers in dignified fashion.

"Of course there are horses!" giggled Popsy. "That's what Fleet is — a horse place!"

"Fleet breeds the best horses in Dorne," FitzFee agreed, sighing for some reason as he turned his head to look at the spirited animals. "The best horses in the whole Sea of Serpents, some say!"

"Is that why you have come here, Master FitzFee?" Sonia asked eagerly. "To trade for a new horse?"

"Not likely!" FitzFee laughed. "The FitzFees do well enough, but we couldn't afford a Fleet horse. Not in a thousand years."

He clicked his tongue to his old brown mare and guided the cart off the road and into the bustling main street of the town. The mare, who seemed to know very well what she was doing, stopped on a paved area that lay before a large, handsome wooden building.

A small crowd of men and women left their work to greet the visitors. Rye tried not to stare, but he could not help it. The people were all very tall — even Dirk would have seemed average beside them. Otherwise, they looked no more like savage barbarians than Fleet looked like a barbarian camp.

They all seemed tired, but there was a quiet dignity about them that was very impressive. Their garments were work-worn, yet somehow elegant. Despite the shadows under their eyes, they all looked in good health, except for the two youngest — strapping young men of about Dirk's age, whose faces were covered in angry red blotches and blisters.

Everyone was smiling. It was clear that FitzFee had been expected and was very welcome in Fleet. Yet

Rye could sense a sort of tension, a suppressed excitement rising from the crowd.

A tawny-haired man with watchful eyes moved forward, holding a sturdy boy of about eight by the hand.

"Welcome, FitzFee!" he exclaimed. "So, here are our goats! And very fine they look."

"The best I had!" said FitzFee, jumping from the cart and turning to lift Popsy down after him. "Good to see you again, Nanion — and young Nanion, too! Bless my heart, how he's grown! Why, he's as tall as me already!"

The boy grinned, his likeness to his father suddenly becoming very plain.

"I've brought my girl with me, as you see," FitzFee rattled on, drawing Popsy forward. "I fancied she'd enjoy the outing. Her mother's very busy with young Tigg these days. He's teething."

"Indeed," said the man Nanion, smiling at the little girl, who dimpled shyly back.

FitzFee waved his hand casually at Rye and Sonia, who had risen to their feet and were standing uncertainly among the goats.

"And here are two young travelers we met on the road," he added. "They'd lost their way and were having a bit of trouble with a bloodhog, but we soon put that right."

The man Nanion laughed. "I daresay you did, FitzFee!" he said. "Well, please come, all of you, into the guesthouse for refreshments. Serri and Peron will see to the goats and lead your good mare to shade and water."

The crowd melted away as people hurried back to their work. Serri and Peron, the two young men with marked faces, moved silently to the cart. They darted sharp, curious glances at Rye and Sonia, then ducked their heads. Perhaps the ugly red blisters that so spoiled their good looks embarrassed them. Or perhaps, Rye thought, looking down at himself, they were merely being tactful because their visitors were so dirty and bedraggled.

Serri and Peron began unloading the goats. Feeling that it would look strange if they stayed in the cart any longer, Rye and Sonia climbed down and moved rather nervously to stand behind FitzFee.

"All well, I gather, Nanion?" they heard the little man asking in a low voice.

Nanion's lips tightened, but he nodded. "Olt's ruffians came four days ago. They turned the town upside down searching, but finding no one here to interest them, they went on their way."

Rye heard Sonia draw a quick breath, and concentrated on keeping his face expressionless.

"We have been very busy since we were rid of them, as you can imagine," Nanion was continuing. "There has been little sleep for any of us."

As he spoke, he raised his eyes to look at Rye and Sonia. Rye felt a jolt of alarm as the eyes suddenly widened, then turned to glare at FitzFee.

He has seen through the lie, Rye thought, panic-stricken. The moment he looked at us closely he knew exactly who we were.

For a split second, he thought of grabbing Sonia's hand and running. Then he saw that FitzFee was looking shamefaced but quite calm. FitzFee, at least, did not fear that Nanion of Fleet would betray them.

"How could you have brought them here, FitzFee?" growled Nanion. "Dirt and ragged clothes are no disguise! And so close to —"

"Yes, well, bless my heart, what was I to do?" FitzFee exclaimed, holding up his hands as if to defend himself. "Let them walk? They're determined to get to Oltan, and some young people just won't be told, Nanion, as you well know."

"Indeed I do," Nanion agreed, grim-faced. "Well, as it happens, Fleet is safe enough for them now, at least. There is no reason for Olt's louts to return here. From what I hear, their vile mission was completed yesterday — not very far from your farm, either, FitzFee — and they are now back in Nerra."

Hearing the forbidden name, Popsy gasped and clapped her hand over her mouth as if it had been she who had uttered it.

Nanion's face softened, and he lightly touched the little girl's curly head. With a shock, Rye saw that he was wearing a braided ring on his index finger. It was just like the one on Rye's own hand.

What did this mean? Rye longed to ask, but he

did not dare. He had promised FitzFee to keep his mouth shut, ask no questions.

"*Oltan*, I should say, Popsy," Nanion said gently. "How could I have made such a foolish mistake? I will forget my own name, next!"

He looked back at Rye and Sonia, and to Rye's astonishment, he smiled.

"You are tired, young ones," he said. "Tired to death and sore at heart. There is little enough we can do to comfort you, but we can offer food, rest, and a bath, at least."

"A *bath*!" Rye and Sonia both sighed with pleasure at the very idea.

Nanion nodded. "And perhaps a change of clothes might be in order," he suggested, looking wryly at their filthy, stinking garments. "I fear the ones you are wearing are fit only for burning."

An hour later, Rye left the small bathroom at the back of the Fleet guesthouse feeling like a new, smooth creature who had emerged from an itchy, dirt-encrusted shell.

Never had he enjoyed a bath so much. Never had he realized what a relief it could be to be clean. His damp, washed hair felt featherlight, and he had stuffed FitzFee's cap into a pocket instead of putting it back on. His bell tree stick was safely tucked into his belt. The little bag hung around his neck. The clothes he had been given to wear smelled faintly of soap and sun, and were deliciously soft against his skin.

Now all he wanted was food.

Sonia had been taken to another bathroom, he was not sure where. Deciding he was too hungry to wait for her, he began trying to find his way back to the room where he had last seen FitzFee.

The room had been large and airy, built around a great central chimney that seemed to have been carved from a single piece of rock. Savory pies, spiced sausages, fragrant bread, and fruit had been set out on a table there. The thought of them made his mouth water.

He met no one as he moved toward the front of the building, past the open doors of several small, empty bedrooms.

Nanion had told him that these bedrooms were for the use of horse buyers who had come to Fleet from afar and needed to stay overnight before returning home. There were no such buyers now, it seemed. The little rooms had a bare, deserted air. The beds had been stripped of their pillows and coverings. In some cases, even the mattresses had gone.

Rye reached a door and opened it cautiously, not sure if it was the one he had been seeking. He realized it was when he heard FitzFee's voice.

"You're quite set on the scheme, then, old friend?" FitzFee was asking.

Rye opened the door a little wider. He saw the backs of two armchairs drawn up in front of one of the fireplaces that gaped at the base of the room's central chimney. Nanion was sitting in one chair, and it seemed that FitzFee was in the other, though he was too short for his head to be visible.

The two men must have taken these chairs out of habit, because there was no fire. A small, white-furred creature was peeping from the shadows of the empty grate, eagerly snatching up the fragments of sausage that were being tossed to it by FitzFee.

"You'll truly risk your people and your horses on the sea?" FitzFee went on.

"We have no choice," said Nanion. "We can no longer live under Olt's rule — we *will* not! And we learned seven years ago the cost of defying him. Some chose to leave us and hide from him in Dorne, but that was not possible for most of us. You cannot hide horses in the numbers we keep, and horses are our lives."

The hair rising on the back of his neck, Rye took a step back. The two men had no idea he was there. By all Weld standards, he should have turned and crept away. Yet still he lingered, too fascinated to close his ears.

"The ships are ready and waiting to the north, well away from Nerra," Nanion said. "Their captains are helping us for gold, not friendship, but on the whole, they seem honorable. I think they will serve us well."

"But where will you go?" FitzFee became briefly visible as he rose a little to throw another scrap to the little creature in the fireplace.

"The Land of Dragons, to the west, is at peace now after its many years of trouble. We have heard it will welcome us or at least will not object to our landing on its shores and finding a place to settle and start afresh. We can only hope that this is true."

"*Dragons?*" hissed FitzFee. "But Nanion —"

"What are dragons but serpents of the air?" Nanion slapped the arms of his chair. "And what creature, on land or sea, could be more fearful than Olt? FitzFee, stop feeding that clink! If you give her too much sausage, she will not do her job and keep down the mice!"

"Ah, no fear of that," said FitzFee, tossing the little animal yet another morsel. "Clinks are always hungry. And what does one mouse more or less matter to you now? Soon you will be far away, and your clinks will have the whole of Fleet to themselves."

"True," Nanion admitted. "So the wheel turns full circle. Clinks were here long before humans were. Why, Fleet was built in this spot because of the fine chimneys the clink colony had hollowed from the rocks. They will be glad enough to be rid of us, I daresay."

"No. They'll miss the warmth of your fires and the comfort of your scraps." FitzFee paused. "And I'll miss you, too, Nanion. I'll miss you sorely."

"Come with us, FitzFee!" Nanion urged, leaning toward the little man's chair. "Gather up Alda and the children, and come with us! Dorne is no place for decent people any longer."

FitzFee sighed. "You're right, I know," he admitted, "but it's hard, Nanion. Alda feels — she's sure — that things will change one day. She says the people will rise up against Olt in the end, whatever the cost. And of course Tigg and Popsy take after my side of the family, so they're not in any danger."

"They are not in danger *now*," Nanion growled. "Who knows what might happen in years to come?"

FitzFee said nothing to that, and for a moment or two, the two men sat in silence.

"I don't see how you're going to move so many people and horses to the coast without being found out," FitzFee said soberly at last. "Olt might have been happy to be rid of those who are a danger to him. But he will not be so glad to lose the horse magicians of Fleet — and the whole of their breeding stock!"

Nanion leaned forward, gazing at the clink chattering hopefully in the empty grate.

"That is why we have waited till now to make our move. On Midsummer Eve, Olt will be too taken up with his foul ceremony to notice what is happening elsewhere in Dorne — even here, under his nose." He sighed heavily. "It is a terrible thing to profit by the suffering of others, FitzFee," he said. "But the suffering will happen whatever we do. Tomorrow, Olt will wallow in blood once more. And when he wakes the next morning, he will find us gone."

Very quietly, Rye backed into the corridor, pulling the door shut behind him.

THE GIFTERS

Moving as quickly as he dared, Rye tiptoed back the way he had come. His mind was buzzing, but his first concern was that Nanion and FitzFee did not suspect they had been overheard.

Safely reaching the bathroom again, he set off to try to find Sonia. He could not wait to tell her what had been said.

He knocked quietly at every door he came to, but received no reply. Then, without warning, he turned a corner and found himself in a little courtyard garden that was bathed in sunlight and almost filled by the graceful tree that grew in its center.

The sight brought a lump into Rye's throat, for the tree was a bell tree. It had been stripped of fruit and was far larger than any tree was allowed to grow in Weld. Still, it reminded him painfully of the garden at home, as it had been before the skimmer attack.

As he approached the tree, he saw that beneath its branches, close to its trunk, was a stone slab, with another stone at its head. A grave.

Moving closer, ducking beneath the drooping, leafy boughs, Rye read the words carved into the upright stone.

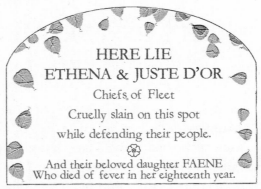

HERE LIE
ETHENA & JUSTE D'OR
Chiefs of Fleet
Cruelly slain on this spot
while defending their people.

And their beloved daughter FAENE
Who died of fever in her eighteenth year.

Rye stared sadly at the carving. After hearing what Nanion had said to FitzFee, it was easy to guess that the deaths of Ethena and Juste D'Or must have had something to do with the tyrant Olt.

The lines about Faene D'Or looked sharper and newer than those in memory of her parents. The young woman had followed her mother and father quite recently, then. And the people of Fleet had felt it right to lay her to rest in the same grave and add her name to their stone.

Rye heard feet on the path that circled the little garden. He turned quickly and pushed his way out from the shade of the tree.

He met the surprised eyes of two pretty young women. It took a few startled moments before he realized that one of them was Sonia!

His mouth must have fallen open, because Sonia's eyes narrowed and she dropped a mocking curtsey.

"You look better, too, Rye," she remarked. "But I am not so impolite as to stare!"

"I am sorry," Rye managed to say, feeling his face grow hot. "It was a surprise, that is all. I have only ever seen you —"

Sonia raised her eyebrows. "Covered in soot, mud, fell-dragon slime, and goat droppings?" she finished for him sweetly.

"Well — yes," Rye mumbled. "I did not even realize your hair was . . ."

Red — magnificent golden red, like the hair of the Fellan. Washed clean and freed from the confining cap, it curled in a shimmering copper cloud about Sonia's face and shoulders.

Knowing that nothing he could say would undo the damage done by that first, astounded look, Rye turned to Sonia's companion.

And she . . . she was beautiful! She was like a picture of a princess in a book of old tales. Her heart-shaped face was exquisite. Her golden skin was perfect. Her gentle blue eyes were warm. Her tawny hair fell down her back in shining waves as thick and smooth as honey.

She smiled with great sweetness. "Greetings,

Rye," she said softly. "I am glad to meet you. Except for your hair, you look very like your brother."

Rye's heart gave a great leap. "You know Dirk?"

"Oh, yes indeed," the young woman murmured, her smile faltering a little. "Dirk was with us for many months. He was very ill at first, but once he began to recover, we . . . he spoke of you often. You and your other brother, Sholto, and your mother."

Rye gaped at her. "Dirk told you about —?"

"He missed you all very much," Sonia cut in loudly. "Because you were so far away. Though he could not say where, of course."

The beautiful girl nodded. "I guessed his home must be on the other side of Dorne — on the east coast. A great many people went there, to escape from Olt. But he had been forbidden to speak of it, he said, and as there were things I could not tell him either, I did not press him."

"Oh." Rye swallowed, appalled at how nearly he had blurted out the truth. How could he have thought that Dirk would break his vow and reveal that he came from Weld? Dirk would never do such a thing, whatever the temptation.

He shot Sonia a grateful glance. She smirked and raised her eyebrows, her eyes dancing.

"Mainly, we spoke of the books I read to him, or the music I played," the blue-eyed girl went on, plainly delighting in the chance to talk about Dirk. "And later, when he was stronger, we would go for walks and visit the horses. Dirk liked the horses very much. He had never ridden one before he came here, he said. I have always heard that the east is a place of high cliffs and wild winds. It is too rugged for horses, perhaps?"

She looked at Rye under her lashes, clearly hoping he would let slip a few shreds of information about Dirk's home.

"It — ah — it is true that there are very few horses where we come from," Rye said awkwardly.

"This is Faene D'Or, Rye," Sonia said, deciding it would be best to change the subject. "The clothes I am wearing are outgrown ones of hers. No doubt you think they are a great improvement on my old ones?"

"Faene . . . D'Or?" Stunned, Rye glanced back at the grave beneath the tree.

"Yes!" Suddenly all seriousness, Sonia hurried forward, pulling Faene with her. "Rye, Faene has been telling me — Rye, we did not understand! We have been wrong, completely wrong! On Midsummer Eve —"

She broke off in alarm as there was a chorus of shouts, and a bell began to clang wildly.

"Beware!" a hoarse voice cried. "Gifters on their way! At the gallop!"

Faene's beautiful face paled in shock.

"Again?" she gasped. "But why —? Oh, Sonia, make haste!"

She and Sonia ducked under the branches of the bell tree. By the time Rye had turned around, they were kneeling by the grave. Faene was pressing the carved decoration above her name on the headstone.

And the slab on the ground was moving! It was sliding smoothly toward the foot of the grave, exposing a long, dark cavity in the ground.

Horses' hooves pounded somewhere outside the guesthouse, and there was a rumbling sound, like cart wheels on paving stones. People were still shouting, and the bell clanged again and again.

"Make haste!" Faene urged, crawling into the cavity and pulling Sonia after her. "Rye, get in! We can make room!"

But Rye knew they could not. There was barely room for two to lie in that narrow, shallow space, let alone three.

"I will find somewhere else," he said rapidly, and backed away, ignoring Sonia's panicking cries. "Make yourselves safe!"

Faene took him at his word. She must have pushed another lever inside the tomb, for the stone slab began sliding back into place. In seconds, the grave looked exactly as it had done before.

Loud, rough voices were bellowing inside the guesthouse now. Rye thought he could hear booted feet stamping on the wooden floors.

Clearly the Gifters, whoever they were, were dangerous. They must be clever and determined hunters, too, if Faene D'Or had to hide in a false grave to save herself from them.

It was tempting to run. With the magic ring to speed him, Rye was sure he could outrun the Gifters as he had outrun the bloodhog. But if he tried to escape, they were sure to catch sight of him. And if they had weapons like FitzFee's crossbow, they would be able to cut him down even from a distance.

Better to hide, then, at least until he knew what sort of weapons they carried.

He swung himself up into the bell tree, climbing as high as he could and crouching among the thick leaves.

It was not a clever hiding place. But games with Sholto and Dirk in the old days had taught Rye that expert hunters often failed to check the obvious places. They expected their quarry to try to outwit them.

He heard heavy feet approaching the courtyard. He clung to his branch, flattening himself against it, as still as if he were made of wood himself.

Six huge young men strode into the courtyard. They wore black helmets that concealed all but their eyes and mouths. Each carried what looked like a slim black club. Each wore black boots, black leggings, and a scarlet tunic with a gold crest embroidered on the center of the chest. Peering cautiously down, Rye saw that the crest was a large letter *O* formed by a sea serpent swallowing its own tail.

"Why have you come here again?"

The voice was Nanion's. He had followed the Gifters into the courtyard and was facing them alone, refusing to be cowed by their size or their weapons.

"Two of the prisoners have escaped the fortress —
freed by rebel scum," the leading Gifter said coldly.

Nanion's steady eyes did not flicker. "I am glad to
hear it. But what has that to do with Fleet?"

"The blood of seven is required. The lost prisoners
must be replaced."

"Then perhaps you and one of your fellow Gifters
could volunteer to make up the difference, Bern,"
Nanion suggested pleasantly. "I am sure there is
nothing you would not do for your master."

The Gifter's top lip twitched. "Gifters serve the
Chieftain, may he live forever, in another way," he
snapped.

"Ah yes, so you do," Nanion agreed with
barely veiled contempt. "You buy your lives with the
lives of others. Yet it may not be wise to trust
your beloved master too far, Bern. If Olt becomes
desperate, who knows what he might ask of your
loyalty?"

"Be silent!" thundered Bern as his two tallest
companions glanced nervously at each other, and the
third, a hefty, round-shouldered brute with a sulky
mouth, shifted his feet uneasily. "We have been
promised safety. The two replacements will be found
in the usual way."

"Then you had better waste no more time in
Fleet," said Nanion. "You already know that there is no
one here to suit your vile purpose."

The Gifter had recovered himself. He smiled

thinly. "We are now not so sure of that," he said. "Perhaps you would care to see why?"

He drew a folded note from beneath his tunic and handed it to Nanion.

Peering down from the tree, Rye caught his breath. Had he and Sonia been betrayed? Had someone who had seen them arrive . . . ?

Nanion hesitated, then unfolded the note. As he glanced at it, he grew very still, but when he looked up, his face was quite controlled.

"How did you come by this piece of nonsense?" he asked, casting the paper carelessly away.

The note fluttered through the air and fell faceup on the moss, not far below Rye's perch. Rye strained his eyes to read it, and fear laid an icy hand on his heart as he slowly made it out.

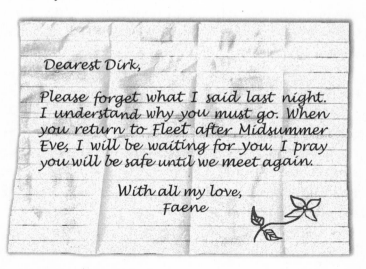

> Dearest Dirk,
>
> Please forget what I said last night. I understand why you must go. When you return to Fleet after Midsummer Eve, I will be waiting for you. I pray you will be safe until we meet again.
>
> With all my love,
> Faene

Numb with horror, Rye looked back at Nanion and Bern.

The Gifter's smile had broadened. He was enjoying his triumph.

"The treachery at the fortress was discovered while the second prisoner was being released. One of the rebels — a savage wielding a giant hook — stayed to fight while the others escaped. Unfortunately he, too, escaped in the end, but his coat was torn off in the struggle. That piece of nonsense, as you call it, was in one of the pockets."

"It must be years old," said Nanion. "You know —"

"It is not old," Bern cut in. "Not nearly old enough." He turned to his companions and jerked his head at the bell tree.

Slightly raising their clubs, the two tallest men marched forward. Rye heard them move beneath the branches of the tree. He held his breath and did not stir.

"Surely the Gifters have not sunk so low that they will do violence to a grave!" Nanion exclaimed.

Cautiously, very cautiously, Rye turned his head a little and looked down.

Through a screen of leaves, he could see the two red-and-black figures standing directly below him, on either side of the grave. They were pointing the slim black clubs at the grave slab.

"Traitor scum deserve no reverence from us," Bern snarled. "But we are not interested in them, as you well know. We are interested in a newer burial. We wish to know how a girl supposedly dead of fever half a year ago was able to give a note to her rebel lover so recently that the paper is still crisp and white."

He raised his voice. "Open it!"

Humming beams of red light sprang from the tips of the black clubs, striking the head of the grave slab and turning it the color of blood. Keeping the beams steady, the two Gifters sidled toward the grave foot. And as they moved, there was a groaning, grating sound, and the slab itself began to move.

Slowly it slid back from the headstone. And little by little, two terrified faces pressed closely together were revealed, blue eyes and green blinking in the sudden light.

THE CAPTURE

The Gifters at the graveside gaped down at their find. "It's not empty, Bern!" one bawled. "There are two of them alive in here! Two! Both perfect! And one's a —"

"Subdue them, you fools!" barked Bern, his voice cracking in excitement.

And in that instant, as Rye tensed himself to leap from his perch, there was a high whining sound, and the Gifters blasted Sonia and Faene full in the faces with bright yellow light.

Nanion's iron control broke. He roared and lunged forward. But Bern was ready. Like lightning, he snatched the club from his own belt and pushed it into Nanion's back. There was a whining flare of yellow, and the big man crumpled to the ground.

Rye froze, seeing all at once that any attempt to attack the Gifters, or even divert them, was doomed.

What hope would he have against weapons such as these? No hope. None at all.

Stay where you are, the voice of reason told him. *Stay hidden. Stay free. You will be no use to anyone as a prisoner.*

So, though it was one of the hardest things he had ever done, he tightened his grip on the tree and forced himself to be still.

"You should have used the blue beam on him, Bern," the Gifter with the sulky mouth muttered, eyeing Nanion's sprawled body with disgust. "You had no cause to be gentle with him. He is a traitor to Dorne and deserves to die."

"There will be time enough for that," snarled Bern, pulling off his helmet to reveal close-cropped brown hair and a shrewd, narrow face. "After Midsummer Eve, when Dorne is safe once more, Nanion will die a thousand deaths. But only after he has seen his town burned to the ground, his people reduced to beggars, and his precious horses taken into the Chieftain's keeping."

He kicked Nanion viciously.

"Bring the prisoners!" he ordered the men beneath the tree. "Take care as you lift them! They must not be bruised or marked in any way."

"We know, we know," grumbled the Gifters at the graveside, bending to their task.

They changed the settings on the handles of their clubs once more and turned red beams back onto the slab to finish opening it. Only when the whole length of the tomb was exposed did they lift first Faene, and then Sonia.

Both girls were breathing, but deeply asleep. Cradling them as if they were made of precious china, their captors carried them out from under the tree.

"Red hair!" gasped Bern, goggling at Sonia as if he was hardly able to believe his good luck.

"So I tried to tell you." The Gifter who was carrying Sonia scowled. "But you were so busy giving orders —"

Bern punched the air, barely able to contain his glee.

"The daughter of the traitors D'Or *and* a copperhead! Both unmarked! What a reception we shall get in Oltan! Ah, never will there be such a Midsummer Eve as this!"

And the Gifters marched out of the courtyard with their prisoners and disappeared.

Shaking, Rye slid to the ground. The grave-shaped hole gaped dark and empty at his feet.

I do not need to chase them, he thought dully. *I know where they are going. They are going to Oltan. When I am ready, when I know more, I will follow.*

He moved out from under the tree, to where Nanion's body lay motionless in the sunlight.

Dirk is in Oltan, his thoughts drifted on. *I have only to find him and tell him that Sonia and Faene have been taken. He will think of a way to save them.*

He crouched and shook Nanion's arm, but the big man did not stir.

"If he was blasted with the yellow flame, he will not wake for an hour or two. It depends how much they gave him."

Rye looked up and saw FitzFee standing at the courtyard entrance, his daughter in his arms and several silent Fleet people behind him. Popsy's eyes were wide and dazed. The small man's weathered face was gray.

"A bad man killed the poor clink dead!" Popsy whispered to Rye. "She came out of the chimney to get a piece of pie I threw. Then a bad man came in and shot blue light at her, and she died!"

Tears filled her shocked eyes and rolled slowly down her cheeks. FitzFee patted her back helplessly, and she buried her face in his shoulder. A young woman with a dark red birthmark covering one side of her face moved quietly forward.

"Popsy, would you come and help me give the horses some tarny roots?" she murmured. "They have been frightened. They want comfort, and they always like to see you."

The little girl hesitated, then bravely nodded. FitzFee put her down and she trotted off holding the young woman's hand. Without a word, Serri and Peron, the two young men who had unloaded the goats, bent to Nanion. Their companions followed as they carried him out of the courtyard.

None of them spared Rye a glance. Perhaps they thought that somehow he and Sonia had brought this disaster down upon them. Perhaps they were simply too shocked and grieved by the loss of Faene D'Or to notice he was there.

"I told you to stay where you were safe!" FitzFee muttered to Rye when they were alone. "Just like Nanion told Faene to injure herself like others her age did. But you wouldn't listen. And Faene wouldn't listen, oh no!"

His blue eyes were dark with pain as they moved from Rye's stricken face to gaze at the gaping grave beneath the bell tree.

"Faene put all her trust in the hiding place this stranger she was fond of made for her before he went barging off to join the rebels in Oltan. And now look! She'll die on Midsummer Eve, and your friend with her."

"Why will she die?" Rye made himself ask. "Why Faene, at least?"

"Are you mad?" spat FitzFee. "You saw her!"

Rye closed his eyes briefly, then opened them again. "Just tell me please, Master FitzFee," he said quietly. "Why will Faene and Sonia die on Midsummer Eve?"

And finally, staring, FitzFee told him. At last, Rye heard the truth that Sonia had learned before him from Faene D'Or.

The seven prisoners to die on Midsummer Eve

were not captured spies. They were simply seven perfect specimens of Dorne youth — seven young people between the ages of fourteen and twenty-four, without a blemish, and in full health and strength. And they were to die so that Chieftain Olt, the ancient, failing sorcerer Olt, might live.

"The sacrifice of seven young ones at sunset on Midsummer Eve will grant Olt another seven years of life," FitzFee finished dully. "The first Gifting was seven years ago. This is the second."

"By the Wall, how is it possible?" breathed Rye.

FitzFee looked baffled. "By what wall? What do you mean?"

When Rye said nothing, he shrugged and went on.

"I can't explain the magic — there is no Fellan in me, I'm glad to say. But Olt's mother was a Fellan, and magic runs strongly in his veins. He created the spell and made the Gifting law. Once he was loved and respected — the greatest Chieftain Dorne had ever seen, they say. Now he's a monster. And while he's got Dorne's young to prey on, he'll never die."

"But — but why do the people stand for it?" Rye stammered.

"Why?" FitzFee looked at Rye quizzically. "Fear, my friend. Fear of Olt's guards. Fear of Olt's power. Not to mention fear of what might happen if Olt dies and the magic circle he weaves around Dorne dies with him."

Still he stared at Rye, his face puzzled. And Rye stood staring back, trying to grasp what he had heard, to make this horror seem real.

"You really didn't know this before, did you?" FitzFee said slowly after a moment. "When you and the girl insisted on going to Oltan, you weren't planning to join the rebels who fight the Gifting, like I thought. You just didn't understand the danger."

"No," said Rye, his voice very low. "We did not understand."

FitzFee shook his head in wonder. "Your parents must have guarded your ears and your eyes very fiercely, friend, if you didn't even know the evil you were escaping!"

"We did not understand," Rye repeated, turning his head away.

He had realized by now that FitzFee had no idea where he and Sonia had really come from. FitzFee thought merely that they were the lost members of a group who had gone into the wilds to try to save their young from the Gifters.

How wrong we were, Rye thought bitterly. *We believed Weld was the center of everything, jealously desired by all. In fact, Weld is only a small, forgotten corner of Dorne, locked away so long that the suffering people beyond the Fell Zone neither remember nor care about it.*

Only Olt remembered Weld — Olt, the tyrant who would sacrifice anyone and anything to clutch at a little more life, a little more power.

A touch on his arm roused him. He saw that FitzFee was looking up at him with pity etched in every line of his face.

"My good lady and I can give you a bed for tonight," the small man said gently. "In fact, you'd be more than welcome to stay with us a while, and help me with the goats. I could do with a hand just now."

"You are kindness itself, Master FitzFee," Rye murmured, his heart very full. He glanced one last time at the bell tree, then led the way back into the guesthouse.

FitzFee followed him in silence to the big room where the two armchairs had been hurriedly pushed back from the central chimney, and the clink no longer chattered in the cold, empty grate.

Rye looked at the food on the table. His stomach heaved at the very sight of it. He pulled the knitted cap from his pocket. He now understood why FitzFee had made him wear it. Like Tallus the healer, Olt clearly thought red hair was a sign of special power.

Because Fellan have red hair, no doubt, Rye thought grimly.

He remembered the Fellan's smooth, serene faces with dislike. The Fellan did not have to fear the Gifting. They were safe in their protected territory — safe thanks to their treaty with the tyrant, who was half Fellan himself.

And that was all they cared about. Edelle was the

only one of them to have a grain of sympathy for the people who lived in terror beyond the Fell Zone.

Rye pulled the cap on, tugging it down till every coppery hair on his head was hidden.

"What are you doing?" FitzFee asked, eyeing him anxiously. "We won't be leaving yet awhile."

"I cannot thank you enough for your offer, Master FitzFee," said Rye. "But I must go on to Oltan."

In vain did FitzFee argue that nothing — no power in Dorne — could save Sonia and Faene. In vain did he tell Rye that no one in Fleet would dream of going after them, because the only ending to such a quest would be disaster. In vain did he rage that on foot Rye would reach Oltan too late in any case, and warn him not to imagine for a moment that he would be given the use of a Fleet horse to make the journey.

"I do not want a horse, Master FitzFee," Rye said, twisting the shabby plaited ring on his finger. "I cannot ride. But I can run."

CITY OF NIGHTMARE

And so it was that Rye of Weld sped with the aid of magic from Fleet to the coast of Dorne in a single afternoon. So he, for the first time in his life, saw the vastness and beauty of the sea that surrounded his island home.

So, just before sunset on the day before Midsummer Eve, he entered the city of Oltan and knew that it was the place that for two long years had haunted his dreams.

Oltan was a maze of blackened stone, a confusion of narrow, twisting streets that seethed with dark and desperate life. People of every shape, size, and color jostled one another heedlessly between grimy, towering walls.

Their faces were wild with excitement, twisted with rage, blank with despair. They cursed and spat, roared their anger, laughed for no reason. Above their heads, hundreds of red banners strung between buildings flapped and snapped in a fresh wind that did not seem to reach to the streets below. Every banner carried the same words.

Witness the Gifting
Midsummer Eve
Olt Must Live!

Lost in the boiling throng, it was at first as much as Rye could do just to keep on his feet. His legs were trembling after his long run, but he was forced to keep moving, he knew not where. Dazed by the noise, the sights, the smells that beat at his senses, he was shoved mercilessly if he hesitated for a single moment to try to get his bearings. And he soon discovered there was no point whatever in trying to keep to the right.

He almost laughed as he thought of the old Weld rule.

There was no keeping to the right here. There was no order. There were no rules. There was only vigorous, pushing, frightening, brawling, selfish life.

Sweating food sellers wearing neither gloves nor clean white caps stoked the fires that kept their pots bubbling while they bawled to the passing crowds to come and buy.

Gaunt men and women crouched on every corner, holding up their cupped palms, begging for coins and crusts.

Drinkers of all ages spilled from the doors of taverns filled to bursting and roaring with heat and music.

Hairy, grinning creatures that looked a little like humans, but plainly were not, shambled through the crowd. Their nimble fingers lifted purses, watches, and even rings from the unwary, and passed the treasures on to the flashily dressed people who strolled casually beside them.

Strange, absurdly colored birds with curved beaks screeched on the shoulders of men with a rolling way of walking and faded, faraway eyes. The men themselves wore gold earrings, and their leathery skins were a patchwork of smudgy pictures that looked as if they had been burned on with a fiery pen.

The air was thick with the smells of stale sweat, hot food, spilled ale, spices, and blood. And pounding through the din of human and animal struggle was a deep, regular booming, like the beat of a gigantic heart.

Rye felt himself being pressed, slowly but surely, toward the source of the sound. It was as if the streets of the city were streams that might wander for a while but at last were compelled to flow to the sea.

And finally the sea lay before him, water and shore, separated from him only by a high metal net fence fluttering with flags. Here was Oltan Bay, broad and rippling, its headlands dark against the reddening sky. Here were white sands where waves made their small thunders and foam ran, hissing, up the beach. Here a grim stone fortress loomed, dominating the shoreline, frowning out at the sea.

Rye looked up at the fortress and the hair rose on the back of his neck. He could feel the evil of a vast, cold, selfish will beating at him from every slitted window, every ancient stone. He could feel it streaming through the bars that sealed the stronghold's gateway like long black teeth.

And he could feel terror, too — terror, pain, and death. Not just from the fortress itself, but even more strongly from the huge, flat-topped rock that rose from the sand directly below it.

Thick iron rings had been hammered into the rock's surface. The rings might have been used to tie up boats, but Rye knew this was not their purpose. A wooden walkway stretched down from the fortress to a square platform just above the beach, then ran on, sloping more steeply, to the top of the rock. Like the fence, the walkway looked raw and new, as if it had been built only very recently.

In readiness for Midsummer Eve.

Just one among hundreds, Rye pressed his face against the fence. He saw the waves crash. He saw the foaming water run up the beach, hiss against the base of the rock, and retreat, leaving clumps and strands of flabby weed behind it. He saw that every time a wave broke, the water surged a little higher, till at last there came a time when it did not retreat but remained swirling gently around the rock.

At first, his skin crawled at this evidence of Olt's sorcery, so powerful that it could even control the waves of the sea. Then he suddenly realized that he was seeing with his own eyes something he had only read about before.

"The tide is rising!" he murmured aloud, tasting the words on his tongue. The man beside him glanced around, his sharp eyes curious, his red, beaky nose twitching.

Fortunately, at that moment, there was a stir in the crowd, and boots pounded on the walkway. Rye's curious neighbor lost interest in him and turned quickly to look.

Men wearing the black helmets and scarlet tunics of Gifters were marching onto the rock, pulling a cart loaded with barrels. Ignoring the breathless, watching crowd, the Gifters began unloading the barrels and tipping their red, lumpy contents over the side of the rock, into the swirling water.

Rye smelled fresh blood. His stomach turned over.

"I daresay they're glad this is the last time they'll have to blood the waters, Dorrie," he heard the man with the beaky nose comment to his companion, a hefty woman eating fried potato chunks from a greasy twist of paper. "I hear one of them slipped and got taken last night."

"Sad," the woman sighed, licking her fingers. "Still, it was his choice to be a Gifter. And the blooding has to be done, they say."

"Of course!" the man said enthusiastically. "The serpents have to learn there's a feed here for them at sunset, don't they? Otherwise, we won't have a good Gifting. They say five came in last night. I've bet on seven for Midsummer Eve. Seven's my lucky number."

The woman turned and peered at the sea. "Looks to me as if there's more than that out there now," she said placidly. "I'd say you've lost your bet, Coop. There'll be nine or ten tomorrow night, for sure."

Cold with horror, Rye also looked out at the water.

The sky was red as blood. The sea was heaving, boiling with white foam.

But it was not just the tide that was making the waters heave and swell. As Rye watched, a great, coiling shape broke the surface. He saw a flash of silver, and the silhouette of a vast, spiked head rising from the foam.

Rye clung to the fence, staring, unable to tear his eyes away. He had seen pictures of sea serpents — of course he had! Even the map of Dorne on the schoolhouse wall had shown serpents swimming sedately in the sea surrounding the island.

But nothing he had seen had prepared him for this first sight of the real thing. The savage, spined head rose higher and higher. The snakelike body — as thick as the trunk of one of the giant trees of the Fell Zone — writhed in great, glittering loops. The monster could have wrapped itself twice around Rye's little house in Weld.

The sea serpent opened its jaws, showing long, glinting fangs. A weird, high, hooting sound filled the air.

It must have been some sort of challenge, because another serpent surfaced almost instantly. This one was a darker color — blue, perhaps, or green. There was another hooting sound. Two sets of jaws gaped wide as the monsters rose even higher in the water and joined in battle, their bodies tangling and twisting horribly against the sky, their tails thrashing the water into froth.

"The smell of blood stirs them up," Rye heard his neighbor say knowledgeably.

Then, suddenly, the waves close to shore erupted in an explosion of spray and snarling jaws. Three smaller serpents had sped unnoticed to the beach while everyone was watching the fight.

Green, sickly yellow, and glittering blue-black, the beasts lunged at the rock, tearing and gulping at the ragged chunks of flesh that drifted in the bloody shallows. As the drenched crowd screamed in a frenzy of excitement and fear, the Gifters leaped for safety, sprawling onto the walkway and taking to their heels.

Hissing, the serpents arched over the rock,

snapping at one another, searching for the live prey that had escaped them by a hair. They snatched at the abandoned barrels, cracked them like nuts, wallowed in the spilled blood, and tossed the remains aside. They struck at the cart, reducing it in moments to a jumble of splintered wood.

Then they turned to defend their prizes as more serpents writhed through the bloody foam, spines upraised to claim their share in the feast.

"That's nothing to what you'll get tomorrow night, my friends!" roared Rye's neighbor. "Eh, Dorrie? Nothing to what they'll get on Midsummer Eve!"

The hefty woman did not answer. Her eyes, fixed on the rock and the fearful, hissing beasts, were suddenly uncertain. Slowly she wiped her mouth with the back of her hand.

Rye turned away from the fence and pushed his way through the crowd, his stomach heaving, his mind filled with confused, shadowed memories.

Glittering coils. Gaping jaws. Blood. Screams of helpless terror . . .

He had dreamed of all these things. Without knowing it, he had been dreaming of the serpents, of the captives, of the rock. And he had dreamed of Dirk, desperate, crawling through stone tunnels, peering into a deep pit.

Make haste! It is almost Midsummer Eve.

He raised his eyes to the fortress, dark against the scarlet sky.

The prisoners marked for sacrifice were in there. He could feel it. And just as strongly he could feel that Dirk was in there, too. Dirk and his band of rebels were hiding somewhere within that dark stronghold. Their plan had been to release the prisoners before the day of sacrifice.

But in all this time, they had only managed to rescue two of the seven. And those two had been replaced.

By Faene and Sonia.

The Gifting ceremony would continue. Sonia, Faene, and five unknown others would die, horribly, chained to the rock. And Olt would live, to kill again, and again, and again.

I must find Dirk, Rye thought frantically. *I must tell him. . . .*

But what good would it do to tell Dirk that the Fleet woman he loved was to be one of the seven sacrifices to Olt's greed for life? What could Rye offer Dirk but pain?

Nine powers to aid you in your quest . . .

Rye raised his hand to the little bag hanging around his neck. And with a thrill of horror, he felt a hot, hairy hand beneath his own.

He yelled aloud, grasped the hand, and threw it aside. He looked down at the sly, long-armed creature beside him. It chattered and gibbered angrily, then snatched the cap from his head and plunged away into the crowd.

Gasping, fumbling for the bell tree stick in his belt, Rye turned to give chase.

"Don't bother," a woman laughed beside him. "You'll never catch a polypan. Just be grateful it didn't get your purse. That's a good idea — wearing it around your neck."

It was the first friendly voice Rye had heard since arriving in Oltan. He glanced at the speaker. She was carrying a basket that smelled strongly of fish but now contained only a few vegetables. Her straw-colored hair was bundled into an untidy knot on the top of her head. Her hazel eyes were lively. He guessed she was still quite young, though her skin was weathered and creased by the wind and sun.

As the woman looked at him more closely, she frowned and glanced quickly left and right, furtively crossing her fingers and wrists.

"I don't know why you're still here, son," she muttered out of the side of her mouth. "But you're mad to be wandering around in plain view. What if the rebels get another prisoner out tonight? Then the Gifters will be looking for a replacement close to home, won't they? Get right out of sight and stay there till tomorrow night's over!"

Out of sight, Rye thought dazedly. *Yes. That is what I need. Somewhere safe, so I can rest. So I can think.*

He looked straight into the woman's worried eyes. "Where can I go?" he asked.

She hesitated, looking at him doubtfully and

186

gnawing her bottom lip in a way that reminded him painfully of Sonia. Then she shrugged, as if she had suddenly decided to trust him.

"There," she whispered, jerking her head to a low building hunched by the shore and surrounded by boats turned upside down in the sand. "Creep in, find a quiet corner, and stay there. Try not to be seen, but if you *are* seen, say Nell sent you. And get that hair of yours covered up again, as quick as you can!"

She hitched her basket higher on her arm and hurried away without looking back.

THE FLYING FISH

Keeping his head down and his hand closed protectively over the little bag, Rye edged through the crowd, toward the low building.

As he moved closer, he began to smell something very unpleasant. He wrinkled his nose. The odor of fell-dragon slime had been bad enough, but this was worse — a sour stench that almost made him gag.

The building was plainly some sort of tavern. The faint sound of music drifted from its lighted windows, but the sandy ground around it was deserted. No doubt the odor kept most people away. A sign swung, creaking, over the door.

Suddenly the door opened, releasing a gust of warm, vile-smelling air. Rye darted into the shadows at the side of the building and cautiously peered back around the corner.

Two roughly bearded men appeared on the step. For a moment, they lingered in the open doorway, frowning at the sight of the crowd still gaping at the serpents thrashing around the rock.

"Look at them!" one man growled. "Gawping fools!"

The other man grunted agreement.

"Well, by this time tomorrow night, it'll all be over, thank the stars," the first man went on, hitching at his belt. "Two weeks stuck on shore without being able to cast a net! How's a man expected to live?"

"The catches will be bad for a while after this, too," the other man grumbled. "Remember how it was last time? Serpents scare off the fish."

"Ah well, we've all given our boats another couple of coatings of repellent while they've been beached," the first man said. "We'll soon drive the beasts off again. Why else has Olt banned us from the water these past weeks? Not for our safety, that's certain. Well, I'm for home, Wilf."

"And me," said the other. "I'm hungry as a clink, but the wife makes me wash before I step into the kitchen. Says the stink of the repellent puts her off her food."

"Funny," the first man said. "My wife says the same, but I can't smell a thing myself."

They walked off together. Rye sidled to the doorway, and slipped through it just before the door swung shut.

He found himself in a dimly lit room crowded with long tables at which scattered groups of men sat drinking and talking.

On the wall opposite the door, there was a bar, where a few more customers stood arguing in low voices as a small, plump woman filled their tankards with foaming ale. An old man hunched on a stool nearby, playing a melancholy tune on a small accordion.

No one had noticed Rye come in like a shadow with the closing of the door. He looked quickly around, searching for a place where he could hide himself away.

A battered piano stood across the corner of the room nearest the door. The table beside it was empty. Perhaps the two fishermen he had overheard had been sitting there, because two empty tankards sat abandoned in the center.

Rye dropped to the floor, crawled rapidly between the wall and the table, and squeezed behind the piano. The corner was cramped and dusty, but at least he was out of sight.

He settled himself as comfortably as he could, then lifted the cord from his neck and opened the little brown bag. The crystal lit up the moment he touched it and he jumped nervously, even though he had been expecting it. He pulled it out, shading it carefully with his jacket, and used its glow to examine the other objects in the bag one by one.

The red feather. The tiny key. The honey sweet wrapped in paper. The transparent disc. The snail shell. The small round nut.

Every one of these things was powerful in some way. Rye knew it. But no matter how long he held each of the objects in his hand, he could not even begin to tell what it was supposed to do.

The only one that gave him any feeling at all was the transparent disc, which again made him fearful and queasy.

Quickly he put it back into the bag. He felt sick enough without it. Even behind the piano, he could smell the rank odor that he now knew was the sea serpent repellent used by the Oltan fishermen. Combined with the other tavern smells of ale and stale fish, it was making his empty stomach churn and his head swim.

After a few more minutes, he began stuffing the other mysterious objects back into the bag, too. They were telling him nothing. He was wasting precious time staring at them. The only thing he had learned was that he had not missed anything when he had searched the bag before.

There was no ninth object. Either something had been lost or stolen from the bag before it came into his keeping, or one of the eight things he *had* found carried two powers instead of just one.

He had to find Dirk! Dirk would help him work out what the remaining powers were. And in the meantime, he had the ring and the crystal to help him.

Then he remembered that he could not even start his search for Dirk until he had something to cover his hair.

Gritting his teeth in frustration, he roughly snatched up the last of the six objects, the little brown nut. And as he did, it broke apart in his hand.

Appalled, Rye gaped down at the two cup-shaped pieces of shell, and the nut's gray contents spilling out into his palm. In his stupid, angry carelessness, he had broken one of the powers!

The shell had split cleanly. Perhaps it could be mended. Gingerly he poked at the gray filling and was surprised to find that it was not firm or sticky, but silky — almost like very fine cloth.

Balancing the light crystal on his knee, he took a pinch of the silky stuff between his fingertips and pulled.

It *was* cloth — the finest cloth he had ever seen or imagined. And as he held it up, he saw that it had been sewn into a shape, as if it were some sort of very simple bag, or . . .

A hood!

With shaking fingers, Rye slipped the hood on. It was a little large for him, and probably looked rather strange, but what did that matter? Many people in the streets of Oltan looked strange.

The important thing was, it covered his treacherous red hair. And the strings that fastened under his chin would stop the hood being snatched off by a thieving polypan or blown back by the wind.

Perfect!

Did this mean — could it mean — that the little nutshell actually had the power to grant wishes?

His heart pounding with excitement, Rye fitted the halves of shell together and wished fiercely for something to eat. But when he pulled the halves apart again, there was nothing to be seen inside.

Disappointed, he was just about to try again when there was the sound of voices close by, and benches scraped on the floor. Someone — two men, by the sound of it — had sat down at the table beside the piano. Rye stayed still, hardly daring to breathe.

"That's better!" a deep, angry voice rumbled. "If I'd stayed at the bar, I'd have ended up wiping the floor with one of them. Buffoons! Glad that the Gifters found two replacements so quickly! Jabbering on about the rebels being spies and traitors!"

"Ah well," a lighter voice soothed. "They're just —"

"Seven young ones are going to *die* out there tomorrow night, Shim!" the first man spat. "And it won't be a clean, quick death, either."

"Makes you sick," Shim agreed. "If life was fair, there'd be another way. But there's *not* another way, Hass, by all accounts. And Olt's sorcery is our protection — our only protection — against invasion by the enemy. Olt has to live, for all our sakes."

"Sometimes I wonder," the man called Hass muttered.

"What?"

"Sometimes I wonder if any invader could be worse for us than Olt. And sometimes I wonder if the danger of invasion isn't just a tale Olt uses to make us let him do what he wants."

"Bite your tongue, Hass!" Shim hissed in what sounded to Rye like real panic. "Don't go saying things like that!"

"I wouldn't say them but to you and Nell," Hass said grimly. "And neither of you is going to report me for treason, I hope. Shim, you don't have any children, but I do. Seven years from now there'll be another Gifting, and my boy will be fifteen!"

Shim mumbled in reply, his voice very low.

Straining his ears to hear, Rye bent forward. The light crystal rolled off his knee and fell onto the floor with a clunk. He scrabbled for it frantically and just managed to catch it before it rolled under the piano and out of his reach.

"What was that?" Shim exclaimed.

Rye froze, his head down, his body awkwardly twisted, one hand on the floor, the hand that held the crystal pressed against the back of the piano.

He was badly off balance, but he did not dare to move. Sweat broke out on his forehead.

"Mouse," Hass grunted.

"Sounded too big for a mouse."

"Rat, then. Clink, even. Who cares? As I was saying —"

"Hass, we all hate the Gifting, but you've got to face facts!" Shim broke in furiously. "You *know* there's an enemy across the sea. You know who he is. You know he's been waiting his chance to come back and take revenge on Dorne, for choosing Olt as Chieftain instead of him!"

Startled, Rye raised his head. And to his utter astonishment, he found himself staring straight through a round hole in the piano, at two men sitting glaring at each other across the table.

One of the men — Hass, Rye guessed — was powerfully built, and had an untidy shock of black hair. He was looking moodily around, his chin propped on his hand. The other, Shim, was wiry, sandy-haired, and freckled. As Rye watched, Shim tipped his tankard and drank thirstily.

Rye blinked, dumbfounded. The hole he was looking through was like a small, round window — but a window that worked only one way, it seemed, for if it had been visible, the men would surely have seen it.

The clear space had slightly hazy edges and had appeared just above the place where Rye's hand pressed against the back of the piano.

The hand that held the light crystal! Rye's heart gave a great thud.

"Well, Hass?" the sandy-haired man demanded, slamming his tankard down. "Do you know it or don't you?"

"I know that's the story," Hass growled, looking back at him. "What I doubt is that it's true. Why should this Lord of Shadows in the west be Verlain? Verlain left Dorne centuries ago. He's surely dead by now."

"Why should he be?" Shim asked. "Olt's the older brother, and he's alive, isn't he?"

"Only by foul means — and the Gifting is the latest and foulest of all."

"Well, if Olt's found a way, the other has, too. They're both great sorcerers — and half Fellan, remember!"

"Maybe," Hass admitted reluctantly. "But even if Verlain lives — even if he and the Lord of Shadows are one and the same — why should he be a threat to us? There are plenty of other lands to conquer — much greater, richer lands, too. Why should he care a straw about Dorne after so long?"

"Oh, he cares," Shim said, his freckled face very grim. "He doesn't forget, any more than Olt does. He's out there, full of hate, and he's grown very powerful. By the stars, man, how can you doubt it? You've heard the sailors' stories!"

Hass snorted. "You're mad if you believe sailors' tales. They'll tell you about sunken singing islands, and people that are half fish, and dragons that speak, and great ghost bells that ring when death approaches a ship . . . they'll tell you anything!"

"That's as may be," Shim said earnestly, "but the Lord of Shadows is real enough. What's more, nothing has been heard of him since his defeat in the Land of Dragons, where by all reports he was repelled by a magic more powerful than his own."

"And what's that to us?" Hass demanded.

"He's angry, Hass!" cried the other, forgetting to keep his voice down. "He was cheated of what he dearly wanted. Wouldn't that turn his mind back to Dorne, the place that first rejected him?"

Hass drained his tankard and wiped his mouth with his sleeve, shaking his head in disgust.

"It's true!" Shim persisted, leaning across the table. "For all we know, his spies are among us now! And what about the other brother? The youngest? He's been exiled from Oltan, maybe, and we were all told to forget his very name, but everyone knows he's still in Dorne."

"He swore to stay away. He wouldn't —"

"He might do anything! Seven years is a long time to be freezing your rear end off on a windy cliff when you're used to the good life. He might have sent word to Verlain that Olt is weakening and near to death. For all we know, Hass, Verlain's warships are waiting out of sight on the other side of the island this very moment, in the hope that the Gifting will fail!"

Rye stiffened. The movement was slight, but it was enough to make him lose his balance. The hand clutching the crystal slipped, and as the magic window vanished, his head and shoulder hit the back of the piano, which jangled softly.

"That's no clink!" Shim exclaimed. "Someone's spying on us!"

There was a scrape and a thump as he jumped up. In two strides, he had reached the piano and was peering behind it.

His furious face stared in at Rye. Rye waited, dry-mouthed, to be seized by the collar and dragged out into the light.

But to his amazement, this did not happen. Shim seemed to be looking straight through him.

"Well, what is it?" Hass called impatiently.

Shim made a puzzled face, rubbed his stubbly chin, then backed away, out of Rye's sight.

"There's no one there," Rye heard him say. "I could have sworn I heard a thud — a jingling sort of thud. I must have been imagining things."

"No," Hass rumbled. "I heard it, too. We'll see about this!"

Again a bench scraped. And the next moment, a big hand was pulling the piano away from the corner, exposing Rye to the whole room.

Rye crouched against the wall, not daring to move as Hass frowned down at him. But then the man's eyes slid over and past him without the slightest change of expression.

"Hoy!" the woman behind the bar shouted. "Hass! What are you playing at?"

By now, every face in the room had turned in Rye's direction. Everyone seemed to be looking at him.

But plainly, no one could see him, any more than Hass and Shim could.

I am invisible, Rye thought, his heart thudding wildly. I am actually . . .

Slowly, very slowly for fear of making some tiny sound that might alert Hass, he lifted his hand to touch the silky hood that covered his head.

The hood was the cause of the miracle — of course, it had to be! Somehow, though it actually covered only part of him, its power veiled him completely.

"Push that piano back where it belongs, you villain!" the woman at the bar shouted, shaking her fist at Hass, only half in fun. "And if you've damaged it, there'll be trouble! That was my gran's, that piano!"

"Sorry, Mag!" Shim called hastily, his face reddening. "We thought we heard a clink."

The woman looked outraged. "A clink?" she snapped. "There are no filthy clinks in my tavern!"

The fishermen at the tables and at the bar laughed and turned back to their conversations. Hass, looking sullen, pushed the piano back into its proper place with the scarlet-faced Shim hovering around him, trying to help.

But by that time, Rye had slid silently out of the dusty corner and was halfway to the door.

THE FORTRESS

It was growing dark as Rye walked quietly up the rocky track that led to the fortress gate. Looking down, he could see that the tide had overtaken the great flat-topped rock. The ominous iron rings and the remains of the Gifters' cart were hidden under foaming water. The walkway was deserted. The serpents had gone.

Rye could have made the climb in moments if he had used the magic ring. But he had not used the ring. He knew that he must not make a sound, or set a stone falling, in case he betrayed his presence.

People were still milling around near the metal net fence, but he had threaded his way through them unseen. He moved up the track in the same way. Softly, disturbing nothing, like a ghost.

He had no idea of what he was going to do when he reached his goal. Light-headed with hunger and shock, he just walked, watching his feet. His mind was wholly occupied with the wonders of the crystal and the hood, and what Dirk would say about them when he saw them.

To be able to see through solid objects! To be able to make yourself invisible! No two powers could be so perfectly suited to a rescue. For the first time, Rye genuinely rejoiced that the little bag had come into his possession. Whoever it had been meant for could surely not have needed it more than he did now.

He had no plan, but when at last he reached the barred gate, he found he did not need one. The hood, and lucky chance, made his way easy.

Two solidly built middle-aged soldiers armed with swords were guarding the gateway. They stood rigidly at attention but looked tired and irritable. Rye could almost feel their longing to sit down, put away their weapons, and take off their boots.

As he hovered in front of them, trying to think of a way to trick them into opening the gate, there was the sound of marching feet in the courtyard, and the iron bars began to rise.

"About time, too!" the stouter of the two guards muttered out of the corner of his mouth. "The night guards should have been here half an hour ago."

"They may not be coming even now, Chanto," his companion muttered back. "It may be something else. There are many more than two men in there, by the sound of it."

As Rye moved quickly to one side, a small army of Gifters swung through the gateway. Each man was carrying one of the thin black weapons that could be adjusted to search, to stun, or to kill. At the head of the band was Bern, the Gifter Rye had last seen in Fleet.

Bern stopped and barked an order. The other Gifters began arranging themselves in a double line right across the front of the fortress.

"Hoy, what's this?" the guard Chanto demanded, catching roughly at Bern's arm. "Gifters don't guard the gate!"

"Tonight they do," snarled Bern, shaking him off. "And they guard the prisoners in the holding pit as well. The Chieftain has decided that tonight's too important to be left to a gaggle of old men."

Chanto's face went scarlet. "How dare —" he began, but Bern cut him off by thrusting a paper into his hands.

"Read for yourself!" Bern snapped.

He stalked back into the courtyard. At once, the gate rattled ominously and began to slide down.

"Better shake your tails, old men," one of the Gifters shouted. "You'll be locked out next!"

The other Gifters laughed and nudged one another as the angry soldiers hurriedly ducked under the closing gate, with Rye at their heels.

Bern had already disappeared from view. The courtyard, swept clean and lined with many archways leading into dimness, was deserted.

"Look at that, Nix!" Chanto muttered, passing the paper Bern had given him to his companion.

As the other guard glanced over the paper, Rye read it, too.

SPECIAL ORDERS:
FORTRESS SECURITY

ALL FORTRESS SOLDIERS ARE HEREBY RELIEVED OF DUTY FROM 30 MINUTES AFTER SUNSET THIS DAY UNTIL SUNSET ON MIDSUMMER EVE.

DURING THIS TIME, FORTRESS SECURITY WILL BE IN THE HANDS OF MY TRUSTED GIFTERS. LED BY GIFTER BERN, WHO HAS PROVED TO BE A MAN OF OUTSTANDING TALENT AND LOYALTY, THEY WILL ENSURE THE SAFETY OF THE SEVEN CHOSEN ONES IN THE HOLDING PIT.

SOLDIERS AND FORTRESS SERVANTS ARE TO REMAIN WITHIN THEIR OWN QUARTERS. THE COURTYARD AND ALL OTHER PARTS OF THE FORTRESS ARE FORBIDDEN TO THEM UNTIL THE BELL SOUNDS TO SUMMON THEM TO THE GIFTING CEREMONY TOMORROW.

THE GIFTERS HAVE MY AUTHORITY TO KILL ON SIGHT SHOULD THEY DISCOVER ANYONE DISOBEYING THIS INSTRUCTION.

"Well, well," the soldier called Nix murmured.

"Is that all you can say?" Chanto whispered angrily. "Don't you see what it means? Olt suspects the Fortress soldiers of being in league with the rebels! It's outrageous! Why, I've served him faithfully for thirty years and more! And he prefers to trust those Gifter louts —"

"Those louts have no doubts about the Gifting," Nix muttered, gesturing at the helmeted men lounging outside the barred gate. "But many of us do. And Olt must know it."

Chanto shook his head. "We may not like the Gifting, but we accept it's necessary. We do our duty, as we always have, for the good of Dorne."

"Perhaps," Nix said. "But Olt's taking no risks."

"If you ask me, he's taking a very great risk!" Chanto exclaimed. "The Gifters are untrained hooligans! And it's pointless using so many men to guard the gate! The captain has told Olt over and over! The rebels have found another, secret way into the fortress — a tunnel or somesuch."

Your captain is right, Chanto, Rye thought, remembering his dreams of Dirk crawling through a low stone passage. And *you* are right. Olt is taking a big risk, depending on the gate to keep the rebels out.

"True, we haven't been able to find any tunnel," Chanto was going on. "But how else did they get to the holding pit last night? How else did they save those two prisoners and escape themselves?"

"Olt prefers to think they did it with the help of a traitor in our ranks," his companion said with a shrug. "Forget it! Time will tell if he's right or not."

"Time will tell?" Chanto raged. "What are you saying, Nix? What if the rebels attack again tonight? And we are all locked inside, forbidden on pain of death to leave our quarters?"

"Then the Gifters guarding the holding pit will have their chance to show what they're made of, won't they?" Nix drawled. "It won't be our business to stop the prisoners being saved. And frankly, I'm glad of it. Come inside, Chanto. We aren't supposed to be here."

He took Chanto's arm and hustled him through one of the archways to the right. A low buzz of talk drifted to Rye's ears as a door beyond the archway was opened. Then the door slammed, and there was silence, except for the sound of the sea on the rocks.

Rye stood alone, looking uneasily from side to side. He had somehow assumed that once he was inside the fortress he would sense Dirk's whereabouts.

Now he knew this was not true. He felt nothing — nothing at all.

Desperately he looked around, trying to find some sort of sign. And then he saw a small glint of blue on the cobbles just in front of one of the archways to his right.

He hurried toward the speck of blue, bent to it, and picked it up.

It was a smooth, round pebble.

A picture of Sonia flooded Rye's mind — Sonia filthy with soot, mud, and fell-dragon slime, crouching to scoop up a handful of pebbles from the swiftly running water of the Fell Zone stream.

I like them, she had said defiantly when she caught Rye watching her. As if she expected him to think she was being foolish — childish, even.

Rye's throat tightened painfully. He stared down at the little pebble in his hand.

So Sonia had kept the pebbles with her when she had changed her clothes in Fleet. They had been carried with her to the fortress when she was captured. And as she was carried through this archway, one had fallen from her pocket.

It was a miracle it had not been swept up along with all the dust, sand, straw, and other rubbish that had been tramped into the courtyard that day.

Then Rye would never have seen it.

It would not really have mattered anyway, Rye told himself. *Dirk will know where Sonia is — where all the prisoners are. It is Dirk I have to find.*

Yet somehow he could not just ignore the blue pebble. He could not.

He moved through the archway, and listened. He could hear nothing — not a footstep, not a voice. As his eyes adjusted to the dimness, he slowly made out stone steps rising in the shadows ahead of him, and another set of steps to his left, going down.

A dank smell of rusting iron, mold, and damp,

ancient stone rose like a vapor from the darkness of the left-hand steps. The smell was horribly familiar. It was the odor that had accompanied Rye's dreams of Dirk crawling through rock, peering down into a deep stone pit, whispering anxiously of Midsummer Eve.

The holding pit was below, Rye felt it in his bones. At the bottom of the stone steps, he would find Sonia, with the other prisoners.

And at last he would find Dirk as well. For later, when the fortress was wrapped in sleep, Dirk and his rebel band would surely come creeping out of their secret tunnel to make a final, desperate effort to save the seven marked for sacrifice.

But Rye had only gone a little way down the left-hand stair when he stopped. Something was telling him that he was making a mistake.

He frowned, trying to make himself move on, but the feeling would not leave him.

Slowly he turned and went back up to ground level. He moved forward, to the set of steps that led upward.

Lying on the bottom step, almost invisible in deep shadow, was another blue pebble. And higher, on the third step, there was yet another.

Rye's skin prickled.

This was no accident. This was no coincidence. The blue pebbles were for him. Sonia had known Rye would come after her. So she had left him a trail.

And for some reason, she had been taken upstairs, instead of down to the holding pit.

The holding pit was where Dirk would come. But Dirk's plans were nothing to Sonia. Dirk had not been her companion since she left Weld. Dirk had not rescued her from the fell-dragon's net, or hidden with her in the goat shed while the bloodhog prowled, or seen her snatched from the false grave in Fleet.

But Rye had. And now, in this most terrifying of all her trials, Sonia was trusting in Rye, hoping against hope that he could help her.

Rye knew he could not betray that trust. He picked up the pebbles and began to climb.

He found a fourth pebble, and a fifth, but after that the darkness on the stair became so complete that he could not see his hand in front of his face. He stopped, fumbled in the little bag hanging around his neck, and brought out the light crystal.

At first, the crystal flashed brightly, too brightly for safety, but he soon learned to keep it masked with his fingers so that only a dull glow shone on the steps ahead.

Spaces between pebbles lengthened, but every now and then, he would spy one and add it to the growing collection in his hand. With every stone he found, the feeling that Sonia was ahead grew stronger.

He climbed until his legs trembled beneath him. He climbed till he at last recognized how hungry and thirsty he was, and bitterly regretted that he had not forced himself to eat and drink in Fleet.

But at last, the steps ended, and Rye found himself standing on a broad landing, facing a stone wall and an iron door streaked with rust.

In front of the door lay two blue pebbles.

No message could be clearer, and as Rye picked up the pebbles, he knew that whatever Olt's notice to his guards had said, Sonia was up here, behind that heavy, rust-stained door.

He pressed the light crystal against the iron and slowly a flickering, misty window appeared.

The window was not nearly as clear as the one in the tavern had been. Wondering nervously if the crystal's power was wearing out and if this meant that the hood of concealment would also soon stop working, Rye squinted through the haze, into the room beyond the door.

A wave of heat flooded through him.

He saw a great, snarling silver head crowned with spines. Below the head, a glittering snakelike body coiled rigidly to make a savage throne. And on the throne, in the embrace of the lifeless but magically preserved serpent, sat a shrunken shadow of a man, wizened as an old, forgotten bell fruit long after summer had passed.

Rye knew that this was Olt.

THE CHIEFTAIN

Nodding inside the white-furred hood of his purple velvet cloak, Olt's face was like a death's head. His thin, seamed lips had shrunk back from his yellowed teeth. His skin hung over his bones, blotched with rough, gray-green patches that looked like fungus. His hands, clutching the coils of his bizarre throne, were like the hands of a skeleton.

But his sunken eyes, ringed in shadow, were burning. And they seemed to be looking straight at Rye.

The door clicked and began to creak open. Rye jumped aside, muffling the light crystal under his jacket, his heart crashing in his chest.

Bern the Gifter appeared in the doorway. He had taken off his helmet, but his black club was in his hand. He looked around the landing. Flattened against the wall, Rye crossed his fingers and wrists.

"There's no one here, my Chieftain," Bern said.

"I felt a presence," a cracked voice whispered. "Look again!"

Bern frowned down the steps, then glanced around the landing once more.

"There's no one here, my Chieftain," he repeated, turning back into the room. "Perhaps you felt one of the prisoners waking. The two new ones were definitely regaining consciousness when we arrived. Shall I . . . ?"

Eagerly he raised the black club.

"No!" Olt rasped. "Leave them! I have control of them. You are far too free with your scorch, Bern! Thanks to you, one of the sacrifices is damaged. Only look at her!"

Rye caught his breath. Sonia! Without considering the danger, he whirled around and pressed the crystal to the wall. Instantly the stones seemed to dissolve before his eyes, and he had a clear, sharp view of another part of Olt's chamber.

One part of his mind registered with relief that the crystal was not failing after all and that iron must simply lessen its power. The rest of his attention was fixed on what he was seeing.

The stiff, glittering coils of Olt's sea serpent throne were to the right of the picture now. Not far beyond them, seven figures lay in line. Their eyes were closed. They floated a handbreadth above the floor, as straight and rigid as if they were suspended on invisible wires.

There were three males and four females. Sonia was one of them. She lay beside Faene D'Or, the fiery golden red of her hair trailing on the stones, which seemed to be spattered with gleams of light.

Rye gaped at the seven floating figures, trying to accept what he was seeing.

The prisoners were here, in Olt's chamber! But they were supposed to be in the holding pit in the dungeons. The notice given to the guards on the gate had clearly stated it.

Most of the seven might have been asleep in their own beds, so peacefully did they lie. Only Sonia's face showed signs of tension. Only her eyelids flickered, as if she was trying to resist the spell that held her motionless in a charmed sleep.

Rye's heart was wrung. It was terrible to see Sonia still fighting, trying to open her eyes as if this would give her some control over what was happening to her.

Sonia, I am here! he tried to tell her in his mind. *I have found you! Do not despair!*

Sonia's brow wrinkled slightly. And Rye thought that for a moment the lines of strain on her face lessened, almost as if she had heard him.

Olt's breathy, rasping voice floated through the open door, cutting through his thoughts.

"The scrawny one was badly weakened by her second scorching. See for yourself!"

A skeletal hand, rattling with loose gold rings and horribly patched with gray-green, appeared in

Rye's view over the serpent coils. It was gesturing not at Sonia but at the smallest of the floating prisoners.

The girl looked frail as a bird. Her short black hair was dull and lifeless. Her eyelids were veined with blue. Her mouth hung a little open, showing small, crooked teeth, and her skin was bleached to the color of old parchment.

"I had to scorch her a second time, my Chieftain," Bern was whining. "We had no choice. She tried to escape when we moved her from the pit."

Hearing the fear in his voice, Rye reflected grimly that the swaggering Bern was a very different man when he was dealing with his master.

"The second dose would not have harmed her if she had not been scorched too heavily when she was first taken!" snapped Olt.

"I'm sorry, my Chieftain," Bern mumbled. "As I told you, the girl was hiding in a goat house, behind the beasts. Several scorch beams meant for the animals hit her instead. It was an error. The men responsible have been punished."

Rye stared at the small, black-haired girl floating helplessly just above the ground, her arms crossed on her chest. Words scratched over and over again on a rough stone wall came vividly into his mind.

How long had this young girl hidden herself in that lonely shelter, scratching her plea on the wall over and over again as if it were a talisman that could keep her safe? Hours? Days? Weeks?

And it had all been for nothing. The Gifters had found her — felled her goats and dragged her out of her hiding place like a stalker bird plucking a snail from its shell.

Olt's hand made an impatient gesture and fell heavily onto the serpent coils that formed the arm of the throne. Silver scales pattered to the floor like rain, to join the other gleaming fragments scattered there.

Dimly, Rye realized that the magic that preserved the serpent was beginning to fail. Just as the magic that preserved Olt himself was failing. The sorcerer and the symbol of his power were disintegrating together.

"The girl was not worth taking in any case!" snarled Olt. "She is a miserable specimen! Plain, ill-bred, and undergrown — barely acceptable! With her heart strained as well, she will be of little use to me. If time were not so short, I would demand a replacement."

"Oh, my Chieftain —"

"But time *is* short, so I will not demand it," Olt cut in coldly. "Fortunately for you, the two you brought to me today from Fleet will make up for the scrawny one's weakness. The copper-head is strong — very strong."

"I knew you'd be pleased, my Chieftain!" Bern babbled. "When I saw her —"

"She is a prize indeed," said Olt. "You did well to find her. And yet . . ."

He paused, and his hand beat softly on the

214

preserved serpent coils, causing more scales to fall. When he spoke again, his voice was fretful and slightly slurred as if he were exhausted.

"And yet, why was she there to find? How could such a one have been left behind? It is a mystery. I do not like mysteries. Yet she is here, ripe for Gifting, and I cannot resist. . . . Bern, look outside again! I feel a presence, I tell you!"

Bern appeared in the doorway, looking uneasy. He gave the landing only the briefest of glances before turning back to his master.

"There's no one, my Chieftain. My Chieftain, forgive me, but I should leave you to yourself. Controlling the prisoners, while at the same time holding the disguise spell over the decoys in the pit, is draining your strength. I'll come back when —"

"Yes," Olt said. "When you have the rebels. When you have them all!"

Rye gripped the wall, weak with horror. Why had he not seen this before? Sonia and the other captives were here because Olt was setting a trap for the rebels! Olt knew very well that Dirk and his band were inside the fortress. He *expected* them to make another attack on the holding pit. He was determined to capture them, once and for all.

I must warn them, Rye thought frantically. *Somehow I must find them, and tell them. . . .*

But he did not dare move. Olt was already suspicious. The slightest sound would alert him to the fact that whatever Bern said, someone was indeed on the landing, watching and listening.

Someone with access to magic. Someone who could not be seen.

Rye knew that this must not happen. The light crystal, the hood, and the ring were the only weapons he had. If he were to have the smallest chance of helping Dirk and rescuing Sonia, those weapons must be kept hidden from Olt.

"The secret must be kept safe," he heard Olt mumbling in a strange echo of his own thoughts.

"It is safe, my Chieftain," Bern replied. "Except for ourselves, no one knows it but the seven Gifters who carried the prisoners to this chamber, then took their places in the pit."

"And the Gifters guarding the pit?"

"They believe their prisoners are what they seem," said Bern. "And if they die fighting the rebels, we can well do without them. The decoys in the pit are my finest men and fully armed. They know what to do."

"Good. Then all is in place. You may go. And you had better pray the traitors attack as early as we hope they will. As you have so kindly pointed out, my strength is ebbing."

The pale lips drew back even farther from the yellow teeth. More scales fell from the decaying serpent throne.

"The attack will come at any moment, my Chieftain," Bern promised recklessly. "By now, the rebels will have heard of your Special Orders. Their spies are everywhere. They'll make their swoop as soon as they can, hoping to take the Gifters by surprise."

"Then why do you wait here?" Olt muttered. "It may be happening at this moment! Go and see! But take care not to *be* seen. We do not want to rouse their suspicions."

Bowing, Bern backed quickly out of the chamber. He kept his head low until the iron door clanged shut behind him. Then he straightened, and Rye caught a single glimpse of his strained, sweating face as he turned and hurried down the steps, quickly disappearing into the dimness.

Rye followed as fast as he could, his footfalls like dim echoes of Bern's heavier tread. In moments, it seemed, he had reached the bottom of the steps. He glanced through the archway into the dark, deserted courtyard, then plunged after Bern into the foul-smelling stairwell that led down to the dungeons.

Cold sweat was beading his forehead. His mind was filled with pictures of Dirk — Dirk, dirty and unshaven, crawling through a tunnel barely wide enough to clear his broad shoulders, Dirk whispering to others crawling behind him.

No, Dirk! Rye thought frantically. Dirk, turn back! It is a trap!

But as he reached a gallery that overlooked a stone pit ringed with blazing torches and saw Bern smiling in the shadows, he knew he was too late.

217

Gifter guards sprawled unconscious on the floor of the gallery and around the pit. Ropes secured by iron spikes dangled over the pit edge, and the dark-clad figures clinging to the ropes had already almost reached the bottom.

Most of the rebels were making the descent clumsily, like the newest apprentice Wall workers. One was not. One was bounding down the side of the pit with the ease of long practice.

Dirk.

At the base of the pit, seven pale figures stood looking up. Four young women, three young men — exact copies of the prisoners in Olt's chamber. The figures seemed to waver, as if seen through a mist, but Rye knew the rebels would not see that.

They would only see what they expected to see — seven helpless victims they were determined to save.

And so it was that, before he could utter a sound, Rye saw with his own eyes the seven prisoners transform into Gifters the moment the rebels' feet hit the bottom of the pit. He saw the Gifters draw their weapons. He saw the rebels' shocked faces, Dirk's face among them. He heard whining sounds, high and low. He saw the yellow and blue flashes of the scorch beams flying.

And he saw the rebels fall. He saw Dirk, his brother, fall. And he saw Bern leaning back against the dank wall of the gallery, weak with relief, and laughing, laughing, laughing.

MIDSUMMER EVE

R ye heard a terrible cry and realized it had burst from his own throat. He saw Bern spin around, scorch in hand, eyes bulging in shock. Then the scorch was wailing as Bern fired wildly at the intruder he had heard but could not see. Blue light sprayed the wall, just missing Rye's shoulder.

Rye turned and ran. His feet barely touching the ground, he fled up the dungeon steps and out into the courtyard.

The gate was rasping open. The Gifters on guard outside had heard the wailing of the scorches and the muffled baying of their fellows in the pit. They were spilling into the courtyard, racing for the dungeons, pushing each other out of the way in their eagerness to reach the center of the excitement.

Rye flung himself heedlessly through the press of bodies. The Gifters did not notice him. They could not see him. Every man thought it was his neighbor who had pushed him. None of them imagined for a moment that a shadow was rushing through their ranks, half mad with shock and grief.

Bursting out of the fortress into a world of salty wind and pounding waves, Rye hurtled down the track toward the city, blinded by tears and spray.

He had no idea where he was going. He just ran, ran like a wounded animal looking for a place to hide. He ran as if by running he could escape the memory of Dirk's crumpling body, from the scalding knowledge of his own helplessness and failure.

The area before the fence, where the crowd had gathered, was deserted now. Rye saw the lights of the Flying Fish tavern and made for them merely because the tavern was a place he recognized. He stumbled to the corner of the low building, where he had hidden once before. And there, at last, his back to the wall, he slid to the ground.

He was shivering all over. The hood was cold and wet with spray, clinging to his neck and ears. The strings around his neck seemed to be strangling him. He tore the hood off and took great gulps of salty, foul-smelling air. A great wave of sickness swept over him. Moaning softly, he curled himself into a ball, screwed his eyes shut, and knew no more.

When at last Rye woke, he found himself staring into a pair of curious black eyes. He blinked. The eyes

220

disappeared, and Rye heard the sound of small feet running away. He puzzled over this for a moment but made no sense of it.

He was thinking about allowing his eyelids to droop again when he heard more footsteps. The steps were slower and heavier this time, and they were coming closer.

"My son tells me you're awake," a deep, vaguely familiar voice said.

A large figure towered over Rye. It was holding something that smelled delicious. Rye's mouth watered.

"Sit up and take some soup," the deep voice rumbled. "It'll help."

Rye pulled himself up into a sitting position. His head swam, and he swayed. The next moment, a strong arm was supporting his back, and a steaming mug was being held to his lips. He sipped obediently.

Hot, savory liquid slipped down his throat. Eagerly he sipped again, and again. His head began to clear. His surroundings came into focus.

He was in a dim wooden shed that smelled of fish, the sea, and serpent repellent. Golden light showed between the boards of the shed walls, on which tools and fishing nets hung. His boots stood neatly beside the sacks that made his rough bed. The bell tree stick lay with them.

The man crouched at his side had brown skin and thick, untidy black hair.

A name floated into Rye's mind. *Hass.*

And suddenly he remembered everything. The dreamy, comforting haze that had clouded his mind lifted like a veil, and the terrible happenings at the fortress glared at him in all their horror.

At the same moment, he understood what the golden lines of light between the shed boards meant.

With a cry, he struggled to get up, but the arm around his shoulders held him back. He struggled feebly, clawing at the coarse blanket that covered his legs, trying to beat off wave after wave of sickening dizziness.

"Stay where you are, boy," Hass said impatiently. "You aren't fit to get up yet."

"What day is it?" Rye choked. "What day?"

There was a pause, then: "It's Midsummer Eve," Hass growled. "Did you think you'd slept through it? No such luck. There's still an hour till sunset."

Rye went cold. He must have turned pale, too, because Hass's arm tightened around his shoulders.

"You're safe, boy," the deep voice said, more gently than before. "No one knows you're here — only me and my wife, Nell, and our own boy, who was watching over you just now. Nell and I found you, on our way home last night. She told me she'd seen you earlier — told you to hide in the tavern."

He looked at Rye inquiringly. Rye nodded, remembering Nell's worried, sun-browned face.

"But there you were, lying under the stars for anyone to see," Hass went on. "We couldn't wake you.

You lay there like a log. Just exhaustion and hunger, Nell thought, but we couldn't leave you in the open."

"You are very kind," Rye murmured.

He felt numb. Vaguely he remembered pulling off the gray hood. Where was it now? Still lying like a discarded rag behind the tavern? Perhaps by now it had blown into the sea. Or . . .

Another wisp of memory came to him. He looked down and saw that one of his fists was clenched. He forced his stiff fingers open. And there was the hood, pressed into a tight little gray ball.

He felt no relief, only dull despair. An enchanted silk hood that did not just disguise but completely concealed its wearer! A hood so fine that it could be hidden within a nutshell!

It was a miraculous power. Worn by the right person, it would surely have made all sorts of wonders possible.

But what did I do with it? Rye thought bitterly. *I crept, and hid, and watched, without being able to lift a finger to change anything, stop anything, save anyone.*

His mind filled with pictures of Sonia fighting to wake in Olt's chamber, of Dirk falling, of Bern laughing. Fresh misery welled up in him. He felt for the little brown bag under his shirt. Yes, there it was, quite safe. Safe — and useless.

"We didn't dare take you home, so we brought you here, to the boathouse," Hass said gruffly. "That way, if the Gifters found you . . . well, we could just say you'd got in by yourself, couldn't we? Olt's made cowards of us all."

He sounded bitter and ashamed. Rye forced himself to speak.

"You are very kind," he said again, looking up into the man's troubled face. "Thank you for helping me."

Hass grimaced. "We did little enough. But at least you had shelter, and now the danger's almost past. Just stay here, out of the way, till it's over. The Gifters won't come looking. Olt can do without you. We heard there was another rebel attack last night, but it failed. Your fellow prisoners and the two replacements are still in the fortress."

"You and Nell think I am one of the prisoners who were rescued the night before last!" Rye murmured, suddenly understanding.

"Of course!" Hass rumbled, his heavy brows drawing together. "Surely you aren't going to insult me by trying to deny it? Don't you trust me even now?"

He snorted in disgust and felt in his pocket.

"If you were not in the fortress, how do you explain this?" he demanded, holding out his hand.

Rye stared at the object balanced on the fisherman's broad, calloused palm.

It was a paper-thin disc that gleamed silver as it caught the light.

"Where did you get that?" he gasped, his hand flying to the little bag hidden under his shirt.

"It was caught in the treads of one of your boots," said Hass. "I saw it when I took your boots off last night. You've been in Olt's fortress — in Olt's very presence! Where else are sea serpent scales lying about underfoot?"

"Sea serpent scales . . . ?" Rye's voice trailed off as he stared at the shimmering thing on Hass's palm.

He remembered scales showering from Olt's failing serpent throne. Bern must have trodden some of the scales out of Olt's chamber. And one had become wedged in the sole of Rye's boot as he followed Bern down the steps.

As Hass watched him angrily, Rye lifted the cord from around his neck and felt in the little brown bag. The disc that had so puzzled him was still there, along with everything else. He drew it out and held it up to the light, feeling the familiar deep trembling begin in the pit of his stomach. The disc gleamed blue-green. Except for its color, it was the twin of the one in Hass's hand.

Hass's frown had deepened. Suddenly he looked suspicious as well as angry.

"Who are you, boy?" he asked in a low, menacing voice. "Who are you, a copper-head who wears a Fleet ring, yet carries around a sea serpent scale like a precious charm?"

"Fleet ring?" Rye repeated stupidly.

"A horsehair ring, from Fleet!" Hass thundered.

"There on your hand for all to see! Don't act the innocent with me! Who sent you here?"

Rye looked at the shabby little ring on his finger with new eyes. Now Hass had pointed it out to him he could see that the plaited threads were not threads at all, but hairs — hairs from the tail or mane of a horse — a Fleet horse, the fastest of all horses.

Powers to aid you in your quest . . .

He wet his lips, turning his eyes to the disc gleaming between his finger and thumb.

If the Fleet horsehair ring, enchanted, gave him miraculous speed, what might the scale of a sea serpent do if steeped in the same magic?

His heart began to pound.

"Well?" Hass growled. "I'm waiting!"

Rye looked up at him. He saw the furious face, the black eyes narrowed with distrust. He remembered the argument in the tavern, and the lively, curious gaze of the boy who in seven years would be fifteen. He made up his mind.

"I am not a spy, if that is what you fear, Master Hass," he said huskily. "I have no master — in Dorne or anywhere else — who wants to seize power from Chieftain Olt. But I must try to stop the sacrifice of the seven at sunset. I beg you to help me."

And as Hass stared at him in blank amazement, a great bell began to toll.

DARK WATERS

The bell tolled on and on, summoning the people of Oltan to witness the Gifting. And the people were obeying the call.

The eager ones had begun assembling long before the bell began to ring. They stood four and five deep all along the fence, chattering and pointing at the rock, the walkway, the platform, the fortress gate, and the huge piles of bonfire wood that studded the beach above the high-tide mark. Most of these people held smaller versions of the flags already flying from the fence, so that the whole length of metal net was a mass of fluttering red, and Olt's symbol was everywhere.

The rest, the great majority of Oltan's citizens, came only when they heard the bell. They came reluctantly, trailing beneath the snapping banners, to stand in silence behind the eager ones like rocks brooding over a flock of noisy sea birds.

As the sun sank slowly toward the horizon, the space bounded by the fortress road, the fence, and the Flying Fish was filled, and latecomers crowded the streets all around.

Very few people had dared to stay away. Olt demanded their presence, and Olt's word was law.

Having found Rye deaf to his pleas to see reason, Hass had stormed to the doors of the boathouse and dragged them open.

"Only look!" he had snapped. "Remind yourself of the true state of things. Then tell me you are not mad!"

Standing just inside the doorway, Rye could see the crowd and the whole broad curve of the harbor shore beyond the fence. He could see the fortress, dark against the sky, and the wooden walkway leading down to the viewing platform and onto the rock of sacrifice. He could see that the tide was rising.

He stared, his mind filled with the plan that had come to him. The enchanted serpent scale and the silken hood were in his hand. He was shivering all over.

The fence keeping the crowd back did not extend as far as the boathouse. Directly in front of the open doors, beyond a narrow strip of sand, a little jetty stretched into the water, its piers already almost hidden by the rising tide. Here, on the sheltered side of the bay, the waves were calmer than they were in the middle, where the broad white beach faced the open sea.

The waves were crashing on the sand in front of the fortress, and already foam was surging up to the rock. The platform and the walkway were deserted, but not, Rye knew, for long.

"Come to your senses, boy," Hass muttered beside him. "It's begun. The bell is tolling. Nothing will stop it now."

"I must try," Rye said doggedly. "One of the seven is my friend. Another, my brother dearly loved. My brother gave his life trying to save them. And . . ."

And if that is not enough, the powers given to me carry their own responsibility, he thought, but did not say. *They may have been passed to me in error, but in accepting them, I accepted this.*

This . . . this nightmare.

He tore his eyes away from the surging sea. The sky was beginning to color. Time was growing short.

"You have two things I need, Master Hass," he said in a level voice. "All you have to do is turn your back while I take them. No one will ever know that I did not steal them. Whatever happens, you will not be blamed."

"It is not that, boy!" Hass glowered. "Or not only that. I would help you, believe me, if I thought for a moment you could save the prisoners and put an end to Olt's miserable life. But I know it's impossible. I know I'd merely be helping you to go to your own death. I can't —"

He broke off as a chorus of shouts and cheers

rose from the watchers at the fence. The fortress gate was opening.

Grim-faced soldiers marched out of the courtyard, wheeled left, and moved down the road that led to the city, halting and turning about only when the track was packed with their bodies, blocked from end to end.

Standing at attention, the soldiers watched sourly as helmeted Gifters swaggered through the gateway two by two. Burly and menacing in red and black, their scorches at their hips, the Gifters strode down to the platform, then moved on to line the lower part of the walkway on both sides, all the way down to the rock.

"You see?" Hass muttered. "The fortress, the walkway, and the rock are sealed off. There is no way, no way at all, to reach the prisoners now."

"By land there is not," Rye agreed.

Hass tightened his lips. He turned his eyes to the waves thundering in to the shore, and the brown bulk of the rock of sacrifice rising from a bed of foam.

"No boat could reach the rock in this tide, boy," he said grimly. "And even if it could, without being swamped or dashed to pieces, it certainly could not get away from shore again."

"I was not thinking of using a boat," Rye said. "A boat would be seen at once."

Hass gaped at him. "You — would *swim*?"

Rye nodded. "It is the only way."

The torches set around the walkway, the platform,

and the rock burst into blazing life. Bern, his helmet tucked under his arm, stepped out of the courtyard and stood aside, his head held high. Then, gliding through the gateway, gliding a hairbreadth above the ground, came Olt's sea serpent throne bearing Olt himself.

The serpent's snarling head and rigid coils were mottled with black where the scales had flaked away. And Olt, shriveled, blotched, and staring, looked like death itself.

The sight was so ghastly that for a split second there was utter silence. Then Olt's skull-like head turned stiffly, jerkily, and his hollowed, malignant eyes glared out at the crowd.

A small child screamed in terror. Bern made a quick signal and the Gifters lining the walkway began to cheer, drowning the child's cries. The crowd at the fence followed the Gifters' lead, roaring and waving their flags. The people behind cheered, too. They knew better than to keep silent.

Hass gave a low groan and pressed his forehead against the boathouse door.

"Master Hass, you are my only hope," said Rye urgently. "I need a tool that will cut through metal. And I need some of the repellent you use to guard your boats from serpents. Will you help me?"

Hass raised his head and stared again at Olt hunched on his decaying throne.

"Yes," he said heavily. "I know I'll live to regret it, but the Heavens forgive me, I will."

He was as good as his word. Just moments later, Rye's stomach was rebelling at the stink of the vile yellow-brown grease being spread over his chest and back.

"What is it made of?" he asked, wrinkling his nose.

"Kobb skin," Hass replied, bending to scoop another handful of grease from a bucket by his side. "Those long oily strips that grow like a mane on a kobb's back fall out twice a year. They wash up on shore like seaweed. We collect them and boil them down to make the grease."

He straightened abruptly and caught a glimpse of Rye's unguarded face. What he saw there made him blink.

"Kobbs are ferocious monsters of the sea," he explained in a voice that had no expression. "Quite common in these parts. I wouldn't have thought there was a child in Dorne who hadn't heard of them."

"K-kobbs? Of course I — I have heard of them," Rye stammered, feeling his face grow hot. "I just — just wondered why kobb grease repels sea serpents."

"Because kobbs prey on serpents," Hass said, regarding him closely. "Serpents think twice about attacking anything that smells of kobb. The grease is not a perfect repellent, but it is far better than nothing."

"My brother Sholto invented a mixture to repel skimmers," Rye said, thinking only of turning his companion's mind away from his lapse.

"What is a skimmer?" Hass asked quietly.

A heavy silence fell between them.

"Master Hass, Dorne is my home, I swear it," Rye said at last. "But I have spent my life far from the coast."

Hass regarded him thoughtfully. "Then how strongly can you swim?" he asked in a level voice.

"Very strongly, I hope," Rye said, glancing at the scale in his hand. "I will know when I try."

Hass cursed under his breath. Without another word, he stripped off his shirt and wiped the fresh handful of grease over his own chest.

"What are you doing?" Rye asked, bewildered.

"You're off your head, boy," Hass said grimly, reaching for more repellent. "You'll drown in that sea. I'll go in your place."

"No!" Rye cried. "You would be seen! The Gifters would kill you the moment you reached the rock, and the sacrifices would go on!"

"And you *won't* be seen, I suppose?" Hass jeered.

"No," Rye said. And realizing that there was only one way to convince Hass of what he said, knowing that his only way forward was to trust, he shook out the silken hood and put it on.

Invisible, Rye walked to the little jetty. Hass's long metal cutters, strapped to his back in a hastily made canvas sling, were very heavy. The foul-smelling goat-hide bag of grease hanging from his belt was heavy, too. The two together weighed him down.

His bare feet made deep marks in the sand. Above each fresh footprint, the ghostly shape of the cutters flickered dimly in the air, because the cutters were made of metal and resisted the magic of the hood.

It did not matter. No one but Hass, standing, stunned, at the boathouse doorway, was close enough to see these faint traces of Rye's passing.

Rye had abandoned his shirt, boots, and socks. But the little brown bag still hung around his neck, and the bell tree stick was in his belt.

He had left the stick where it lay at first, but at the last moment, he had retrieved it and pushed it back into its place.

The bell tree stick had been with him from the beginning. As a weapon, it had been useless, but it was a symbol of home. It had helped him believe that the time would come when he would see Weld again. He would not part with it now.

He reached the little jetty. The water heaved before him, dark and mysterious, slapping angrily against the old wooden piers, which were encrusted with shells of many shapes and colors.

Rye hesitated, suddenly terrified by what he was doing. This was not the warm, rushing gutter water of Weld, in which a boy could wade, and laugh, and think himself adventuring while facing no danger greater than the chance of getting his trousers wet. This dark, heaving water was part of a great sea where monsters thrived. It was alien to him — alien to all human life.

He looked down at the glimmering scale in his hand. It was such a small, frail thing in which to trust. But then, the braided ring, now back in the brown bag, was a small thing, too, and it had saved him when he had least expected to be saved.

He heard the crowd at the fence roar, and turned quickly to look.

Olt's throne was on the platform, facing the rock. Bern was standing beside the throne, a dagger glinting in his hand. Behind them, seven Gifters were strutting through the fortress gateway, each one proudly leading a prisoner in chains. Sonia was first in line. Her golden-red hair looked like flickering flame as the wind tossed it around her head.

Rye took a deep breath and waded into the water. It was cold enough to make him gasp. He could feel the sting of salt, and the tide plucking at his ankles like sly fingers, trying to pull him off his feet.

Closing his hand more firmly on the disc, he took another step. The water rose abruptly to his waist.

Instantly he felt an agonizing stab of pain in his closed hand. He yelled and snatched his hand out of the water, expecting to see some vile creature clinging to it, stinging and biting.

But there was nothing. And when he opened his tightly closed fist, his stomach turned over.

The serpent scale no longer lay freely in his hand. It had sunk beneath the surface of his skin. Surrounded by a ridge of puffy, reddened flesh, it glimmered in the center of his wet palm, flat and shining, like a burn or a scar.

It had become part of him. The water had made it part of him.

Rye shuddered, fighting down waves of nausea. Even as he watched, the angry red ridge that surrounded the scale was fading and shrinking. In moments, it had disappeared completely, and the scale looked as if it had been embedded in the center of his palm since the day he was born.

On impulse, he lowered his hand into the water again and held it just beneath the surface. The serpent scale brightened. It winked up at him like a gleaming blue-green eye.

And in that moment, Rye's shock and sickness vanished. Energy surged through him. His arms and legs tingled as if cold salt water was rushing through his veins. He felt the tug of the tide, and exalted in it. The wild water ahead no longer seemed fearful and alien, but beckoned him. Its call was almost irresistible.

Forcing himself to stay still, Rye glanced quickly toward the fortress, measuring the distance to the rock. The seven Gifters and their prisoners had reached the viewing platform. The prisoners were being forced to kneel in a semicircle before Olt's throne.

Rye's heart twisted as he caught sight of Sonia. She was already on her knees, being held down by the Gifter standing behind her. Faene was second to last in line but she, too, was already kneeling. A feebly struggling man at the end was being pushed down beside her. Rye looked for the small, black-haired girl Olt had so despised, but could not see her.

He blinked. Surely in Olt's chamber there had been three male and four female prisoners. Now there seemed to be three females and four males.

The man at the end of the line was still resisting. The chains binding his wrists and ankles glinted in the light of the lowering sun as he struggled.

Olt bared his teeth and flicked a finger. The man's body jerked. Slowly he sank to the ground. And it was only then that Rye realized who he was.

The man was Dirk.

Rye took a deep breath, and dived.

THE ROCK

The water was like cool silk on Rye's skin. He cut through it like a spear, feeling its power with fierce joy, knowing he was master of it. He could no longer feel the weight of the cutters on his back, or the pouch of grease on his belt. He could no longer feel the weight of his own body. He was at one with the sea, freer and stronger than he had ever been in his life.

When at last he surfaced to breathe, he had reached the rougher water. The surging, whitecapped waves tried to tumble and buffet him. Rye dived deeper and streaked through them, using their force to speed him, always aiming for the fortress and the rock.

Then the rock was ahead. He could see it through the swirling water, rising like a wall from its blanket of foam. He let the next wave flow over him. Then, when it had spent its fury, he coasted into the frothing shallows.

The great rock was taller than he had realized. Stretching his arms up, he could just reach its top with his fingertips. But a shallow ledge, carved out by the sea, ran right across its face not far above his knees. In moments, he was standing on the ledge, peering cautiously over the rock's flat surface.

The Gifters standing at the bottom of the walkway were startlingly close. The lowest two — the two standing at the point where the walkway joined the rock — were so very near that Rye was almost afraid to breathe, in case they heard him. He also became very aware of the smell of the serpent repellent rising from his skin and feared that, at any moment, one of them would catch the scent.

But the Gifters were not trained soldiers. They were not on the alert. Their senses were dulled by the sound of the sea, the tolling of the bell, and the wind that blew unceasingly into their faces. And they were all looking up at the viewing platform, totally absorbed by what was happening there.

Bern was surveying the ragged line of kneeling prisoners, his dagger held high. He slashed the dagger downward, and instantly the tolling of the bell ceased.

A breathless hush fell over the crowd pressed to the fence.

"Citizens of Oltan!" Bern shouted, his voice echoing over the shore in competition with the beating of the waves. "You have come to witness the Gifting — the renewal of our beloved Chieftain, Olt!"

239

The watchers at the fence cheered frantically and waved their flags. The watchers at the back remained silent.

"Our Chieftain Olt loves all of Dorne's people!" shouted Bern, gesturing at the silent, wizened figure crouched on the serpent throne. "Our Chieftain Olt grieves that young lives must be sacrificed so he may live. But he knows, as we all know, that he *must* live! The circle of magic he weaves around our island is all that protects us from the ancient enemy who wishes to destroy us all!"

Cries of fear rose from the crowd at the fence. Bern waited until they had subsided before going on.

"In his great generosity of heart," he shouted, "our Chieftain Olt has this day released the youngest of the prisoners chosen for sacrifice. He has put in her place an enemy of Dorne. This traitor last night attempted to free the sacrifices, so as to leave Dorne undefended against the evil sorcerer who is his master!"

He pointed his dagger at the kneeling figure of Dirk.

The crowd by the fence hissed in anger. Even the people behind them looked at one another, murmuring uneasily.

It is not true! Rye wanted to shout. *Dirk knows nothing of the Lord of Shadows! Dirk is not your enemy! Your enemy is Olt!*

But he kept silent. The avid watchers at the fence believed Bern utterly, and their minds would never be changed by the shouted words of an invisible stranger. And the people behind, the great mass of the people, were too cowed by Olt and his Gifters to rebel, even now when seven lives hung in the balance and the sorcerer's powers were at their weakest.

Bern flourished his dagger and bent over Sonia. Rye felt a chill, even though he knew from what Hass had told him of the Gifting ceremony that Sonia's life was not yet in danger.

Sonia did not stir as Bern seized her hand, lifted it, and pressed the point of his knife into her index finger. The crowd at the fence cheered as the blood flowed.

With his left hand, Bern dabbed at the wound and turned to smear a line of Sonia's blood on Olt's mottled forehead. Olt's lips moved, muttering words Rye could not hear. Deep in his cavernous eyes, small spots of scarlet burned, like coals glowing in pits of darkness.

Bern turned to the prisoner beside Sonia, took blood from him, too, and anointed Olt's brow for the second time. Again Olt's lips moved soundlessly. The ghastly ceremony was repeated with all the other prisoners in turn. And with every fresh smear of blood, Olt's eyes seemed to kindle a little more, and he sat a little straighter on his monstrous, decaying throne.

When the last blood, Dirk's, had been taken, Bern bowed low to Olt and returned to stand behind the throne. The tyrant's lips were still moving. His burning eyes were fixed on the horizon.

The seven Gifters dragged the prisoners to their feet and began hustling them down the walkway, toward the rock.

Not yet, Rye told himself, as his hands tingled and his heart began to race. *You can do nothing yet. If you make a move too soon, all is lost. You must wait. When the time comes, Dirk will help you. He will see what has to be done. He will lead the others.*

But it was agony to stand there, motionless, with the waves beating the backs of his legs, as Sonia, Dirk, Faene, and the other prisoners were dragged onto the rock. It was agony to watch helplessly as again they were forced to kneel in line. It was agony to see the chains that bound their ankles looped through the iron rings, and locked.

Stay still. You must wait till the Gifters withdraw. Wait . . .

Rye edged across the rock till he was so close to Dirk that he could have reached out and touched him. He longed to whisper to Dirk, to let him know that help was at hand — that together they had a chance.

But he knew he could not risk the Gifters hearing him. And as he stood gripping the edge of the rock, so near to the brother he had come all this way to find, he began to see that any words he might say would be useless in any case.

Dirk's head was bowed. His broad shoulders

were slumped. His chained hands hung limply between his knees. It was as if whatever Olt had done to him on the viewing platform had robbed him of his will to resist.

Rye watched helplessly as Faene leaned toward Dirk, sobbing his name. Faene's beautiful face was wet with tears and with the spray now spattering the top of the rock with every wave that broke.

Dirk lifted his head. It was plainly a huge effort for him to do even that. His eyes were glazed. His skin was gray. His shaggy hair, grown to shoulder length, blew and tangled in the wind. He looked leaner, and much older, than he had when Rye last saw him, marching out of Southwall with Joliffe and Crell by his side.

The sight of him struggling to turn to Faene brought a burning ache to Rye's throat. And when, with a low groan, Dirk dropped his heavy head again, resting it on the weeping girl's shoulder, Rye thought his own heart would break.

But grief and pity were not the only things he felt. There was something else, too — cold, sinking dismay.

He had not realized till this moment how much he had been depending on Dirk. Now he faced it. When he had seen that Dirk was still alive — that Dirk had not been killed in the pit but only stunned — he had felt not only piercing joy but also a huge sense of relief. It was as if a crushing weight had been lifted from his shoulders.

He had thought that when the time came, his older brother would take the lead, as he always had. He had thought that Dirk, quickly understanding the plan, would ensure it was carried through.

Now he knew this would not be — *could* not be. Dirk was too weakened by Olt's sorcery to do anything to help himself or anyone else.

It makes no difference, Rye told himself desperately, as the seven Gifters straightened from their task, glancing uneasily toward the horizon. *I am no more alone now than I was when I thought Dirk was dead. The plan still stands.*

But it was as if his mind's brief, comforting slide back into the habits of a lifetime had weakened him, as the flick of Olt's finger had weakened Dirk. Suddenly he felt unsure. Suddenly he was remembering Hass telling him that it was impossible to save the prisoners, that he was mad to attempt it.

But Hass, in the end, had helped him. As FitzFee had helped him. And the Fellan Edelle. Unsure, all of them, that they were doing the wisest thing, they had still decided to trust him.

Unconsciously, Rye squared his shoulders as if to take back the burden of responsibility he had so gratefully shrugged off such a short time ago.

It was then that he felt a stirring in his mind — a soft tugging, as if something he had forgotten was trying to come to the surface. He had the feeling that it had been going on for quite a while, though he had noticed it only now. And suddenly he knew where it was coming from.

He tore his eyes from Dirk and looked toward the other end of the line, at Sonia.

Sonia's damp, draggled hair was whipping around her head like weed caught by the tide. Her face was pale with dread, but hard and set. She was turning her head left and right, as if she was searching for something — or someone.

Searching for me.

The knowledge ran through Rye like flame. Sonia knew he would not abandon her. She knew he must be somewhere near. Even at this last, desperate moment, she was still hoping against hope that he would find a way of saving her.

As fast as he could, Rye edged back across the face of the rock. He had just reached Sonia when a chorus of shouts rose from the crowd by the fence.

Dozens of people were pointing out to sea. The Gifters lining the lower half of the walkway abruptly deserted their posts and hurried up to higher ground.

Rye looked quickly over his shoulder. The sky was bright orange, streaked with red. The sun was a huge, fiery ball sliding toward the horizon.

And the sea was heaving with more than waves. Long, glittering shapes were undulating through the swell. Terrible, spiked heads were rearing from the water, silhouetted against the blazing sky.

The serpents were coming.

NOW OR NEVER

Screams of terror burst from the line of prisoners. The seven Gifters turned and almost ran from the rock. Their boots clattered on the walkway as they made for the safety of the viewing platform.

So it is now or never, Rye thought grimly.

Sonia had made no sound, but her eyes had widened and darkened. She was staring at the sea, her face blank with dread.

"Sonia!" Rye hissed, clinging to the rock with one hand and unfastening the bag of grease from his belt with the other.

Sonia stiffened. She looked in the direction of Rye's voice, and her shoulders sagged as she saw nothing. Clearly, she thought the voice had been in her own mind.

Rye slung the heavy bag onto the surface of the rock, pulled it wide open, and slid it over to the girl so that it pressed against her chained hands.

"Sonia, you cannot see me, but I am here!" he said rapidly. "There is no time to explain. Smear yourself well with this grease. Then pass the bag on. Keep it hidden. Tell the others!"

The moment he took his hand away, the bag became visible. With a muffled gasp, Sonia hunched forward, pushed her fingers into the foul-smelling grease, and began to smear her clothes wherever she could reach.

She disguised her actions well — very well. From behind, and even from the side, it must have looked merely as if the obstinate copper-head had at last given way to despair and was bowed and rocking in an agony of fear.

Rye hauled himself up onto the rock. It took all his strength to do it, with the heavy cutters dragging at his shoulders. If he had still been carrying the bag as well, he might not have managed it at all.

Lying facedown on the rock's flooded surface, he tore the sling from his back and wrestled the cutters free. The ghostly shape of the cutters glimmered faintly in the weird sunset light, but the kneeling prisoners hid it from Olt and the Gifters. Rye could only hope that the people at the fence were too intent on watching the approaching serpents to notice it.

He hooked the blades of the cutters around the chain that fastened Sonia's ankles to the iron ring. Using the rock to brace one of the cutter handles, he pressed down on the other handle with all his strength.

And the blades sliced through the iron like a knife slicing through butter. Elation thrilled through him.

"Sonia, the chain is cut," he panted. "But do not move yet. Olt must have no warning. Stay till the last minute — till everyone is free, and it is too late for the Gifters to capture you again. I will give the signal."

She gave a slight nod to show she had heard. Then she slumped toward the round-faced boy beside her, as if she were drawing close to him for comfort. She muttered in the boy's ear, at the same time pushing the bag of grease toward him.

The boy started and turned to stare at her, his eyes glassy. Sonia muttered again, urgently. The boy plunged his hands into the grease and began clumsily to smear his knees, thighs, and chest.

Rye was already in front of him, cutting through his chain. As the freed length clanked onto the rock, the boy's whole body jerked.

"Stay still!" Rye ordered. "Till I give the word."

The boy made a strangled sound. He thrust the grease bag at the dark young woman who was next in line, making no effort to hide what he was doing.

"Spread this on your clothes!" he gabbled through chattering teeth. "Then pass it on. Keep it hidden. Don't let them see. The copper-head says. The copper-head has conjured up a spirit to save us! But only if we do as she orders."

"Serpent repellent!" the dark girl hissed. "I could

smell it, but I thought I was dreaming!" She eagerly plunged her hands into the grease as Rye crawled past her, and the cutters did their work.

The powerful young man who was next in line was harder to free. Rye had to try twice before the chain fell away from the ring. And as he wrestled with the chain of the fifth prisoner, a thin, curly-haired boy, he realized with dismay that the cutters had been badly blunted. The curly-haired boy had smeared himself with repellent and fumbled the bag along to Faene D'Or long before the task was done.

"Stay where you are until I give the word," Rye warned as at last the chain broke free.

The boy's mouth opened, but he did not speak. He stared past Rye, blinking rapidly.

Rye glanced over his shoulder, and his blood ran cold. Close to shore, a wave was just breaking in a thunder of foam. The wave swelling behind that was a writhing mass of serpents.

A glittering silver head burst from the churning water, twisting into the air in an explosion of spray. Needle-sharp fangs glinted in the red light. A harsh, hooting sound rang out.

Rye looked back, straight into the terrified eyes of Faene. She was just turning from Dirk, plunging her hands back into the bag at her knees. She had smeared the repellent on Dirk before using it for herself.

Rye clamped the blades of the cutters around Faene's chain, just above the iron ring, and pushed with all his might. The chain dented but did not break.

The crowd at the fence roared. The boy Rye had just freed was staggering to his feet.

"No!" Rye shouted, still struggling to cut through Faene's chain. "Olt will see you! Stay where you are!"

The curly-haired boy took no notice. Wild with panic, he lurched from the rock and began to hobble up the walkway, the cut chain trailing behind him.

There was a cry from above. Olt staggered to his feet. He was tottering from his failing throne, his mouth a gaping black hole, his brow dark with dried blood.

"Stop him!" Olt shrieked, pointing to the boy on the walkway. "There must be seven of them! Seven more years of life! I must have them! I *will* have them! Stop him! Stun him!"

Bern darted to the top of the walkway, scorch in hand.

The scorch whined. A yellow beam hit the staggering boy full in the chest. He dropped like a stone and rolled back down the ramp, coming to a stop where it joined the rock.

"Why do you stand there, you fools?" cried Olt, gesturing wildly at the seven Gifters hovering uncertainly behind him. "Move the sacrifice back into place! See that the others are secure!"

The Gifters hesitated, their eyes on the heaving, writhing sea.

"Do it!" Olt shouted, his voice cracking. "Do as I say, or I will kill you all!"

"Jump!" Rye bellowed to Sonia and the others. "Down behind the rock! Use the walkway for cover! Get yourselves up beyond the waterline! Go! Go!"

There was a confusion of movement as the prisoners scrambled up. Struggling with the cutters, Rye could hear Olt's screech of rage.

He could hear other things, too — a clashing, banging noise and voices bellowing defiance. The sounds seemed to be coming from the fence.

Out of the corner of his eye, he caught a glimpse of what seemed to be a riot at the section of fence that was nearest to the rock. The fence was rocking, and the metal net was bulging, as if it was being pushed by people determined to break through.

Rye caught his breath. Was that big, dark figure at the front of the crowd Hass?

He had no time to think about it. The next moment, a crash drowned all other sound, spray was thick in the air, and foaming water flooded the rock's surface. Dimly, Rye realized that this was the last of the wave he had seen breaking. The serpents were in the next wave. The serpents were almost upon them.

"Leave me!" Faene screamed. "Whoever you are — leave me! Go to Dirk! Save Dirk!"

At that moment, Rye felt the chain give way.

"Jump down, Faene!" he gasped. "Behind the rock! Jump!"

When she hesitated, he pushed her, pushed her roughly. "For Dirk!" he shouted. "Do it for him! He would want it. You know he would! I beg you, go!"

With a sobbing cry, she obeyed him, crawling to the fortress side of the rock and disappearing over the edge.

And then, Olt's frenzied commands and the crowd's roars ringing in his ears, Rye turned to his brother. He hooked the blunted cutter blades around the chain that held Dirk captive. He hurled his whole weight onto the handles and pushed with all his might.

And again, the chain dented but did not break. Rye freed the cutters and tried for the second time.

"No, Faene!" Dirk mumbled, shaking his head and trying to push Rye away. "Save yourself!"

"Dirk, be still!" Rye shouted.

"Leave me, Faene!" Making a supreme effort, so heroic that it wrung Rye's heart even as he yelled in frustration, Dirk knocked the cutters out of his brother's grip.

Rye pushed back the hood of concealment. What did it matter if he was seen now? He seized Dirk's bowed head between his hands and tilted it so that Dirk could see his face. The glazed eyes stared at him without understanding.

"Faene is not here!" Rye shouted. "Faene is safe! Dirk, look at me! It is Rye! Rye!"

Dirk's brow wrinkled in bewilderment.

"Rye," he said slowly. "Rye? But how —?"

Water thundered down upon the rock, beating on Rye's back, sending him sprawling. In terror, he heard the clatter of the cutters as they were swept away.

And as the water began pouring back toward the sea, he found himself sliding with it.

His fingers scrabbled uselessly on the surface of the rock. The serpent scale could not help him now. The rushing water was not deep enough to swim in. It was nothing but a force too strong for him to resist. His feet, and then his legs, slithered over the rock's edge.

Frantically he kicked the empty air. His ears were filled with the sound of rushing water, Olt's squeals of fury, the roar of the crowd, and the hoots and hisses of serpents following the wave, eager to be the first to seize him.

Then, with a jerk, the terrible backward slide stopped. Someone had caught hold of one of his wrists. Someone was holding him fast as the water rushed past him. And as the torrent eased to a trickle, someone was pulling his arm, helping him to scramble back onto the rock's surface.

His mind was full of Dirk. But it was not Dirk he saw when he shook the water from his eyes.

It was Sonia.

One foot thrust through the iron ring that had once secured Faene, chained hands still gripping Rye's wrist, Sonia lay facedown and gasping on the rock. As Rye stared, trying to take in the fact that she had not jumped and run with the others, but had stayed to help him, Sonia raised her head.

Her nose was running. Water streamed from her hair, clothes, and face.

"Come away," she shouted to Rye, scrambling up and pulling him up with her. "The Gifters are refusing to come near. The crowd is storming the fence. We have a chance!"

She saw him glance at Dirk, who was again slumped over, his head almost touching the rock.

"There is no more you can do!" she shrieked. "The cutters are gone! Rye, you must leave him!"

"I cannot leave him!" Rye cried in agony. "Sonia — he is Dirk! He is my brother! My brother!"

Sonia's eyes widened. She glanced at the bowed figure of Dirk, her face twisted in dismay. Then, as she turned back to Rye, she screamed piercingly.

She was staring over Rye's shoulder. He spun around.

The silver serpent loomed above them. Its jaws were gaping. Drops of pale gold venom dripped from its fangs and fell sizzling into the churning water. Its eyes were glittering like cold stars and fixed on Rye.

It was poised to strike, yet it did not strike.

The repellent is holding it back, Rye thought. *It does not quite know what to make of me.*

He knew this would not last, could not last. The serpent could see him plainly. The strong scent of kobb was making it wary, but the moment it decided Rye was merely prey, there would be no more hesitation. He had seconds to decide what to do.

It was not difficult. At that moment, it seemed to him that there was only one decision he could make.

Slowly, he pushed his foot through the iron ring that Sonia had just kicked off, bracing himself against the waves. At the same time, he slid the bell tree stick from his belt and raised it high. He lifted his other hand, too, fingers spread, making himself as large as he could.

The silver beast recoiled, very slightly. *Yes*, Rye thought with grim satisfaction. *This is not how prey behaves, is it, serpent? Prey tries to escape you. It does not stand and stare. Be careful. Take your time. . . .*

"Sonia," he said in a low voice. "Go now! Slowly — very slowly. While it is watching me."

"But you —" Sonia gasped.

"I cannot escape," Rye said, his lips barely moving. "It will strike at once if I try. But if I can just hold it like this till the sun has set — keep it from taking Dirk or that boy on the walkway just till then, the Gifting will fail. Olt will not be renewed, and Dorne will be free of him. That is something I can do, at least."

And you will be safe, Sonia, he thought. *You, and Faene. If you live and Olt dies, then Dirk's death, and mine, will not have been in vain.*

Briefly he thought of his mother, alone and grieving. He thought of his father, killed protecting Weld. He thought of Sholto, questing somewhere unknown, and Tallus the healer, solitary in his workroom. He sent them all a blessing. Then he straightened his shoulders and gripped the bell tree stick more firmly in his hand.

There was a rush in the water before the rock, and a blue-black serpent rose beside the silver one. The silver hissed warningly but did not take its eyes from Rye. Towering above him, it swayed slightly. The blue-black serpent drew back its head and seemed to freeze, its terrible jaws agape.

Behind them, other serpents were coming to the surface. The sea heaved with writhing bodies. Water showered from a dozen spiked heads of green, yellow, blue, and black as they rose against the scarlet sky and hung there, motionless as masks in some nightmarish puppet show.

It was as if they were in a trance. It was more — far more — than Rye had expected.

Is the repellent so very powerful? he thought hazily. Is it because I am refusing to run?

And as he stood there wondering, the sun, like a ball of liquid fire, began to melt into the blazing horizon.

SUNSET

There was a howl from the viewing platform. Rye barely heard it. He barely heard the sound of feet stumbling down the walkway, or the tumult as a section of the metal net fence fell at last, its flags crushed into the sand.

He felt no fear, no curiosity. He stood like part of the rock, braced against the waves, facing the serpents and the setting sun.

And so he did not see what Sonia saw as she turned in terror toward the walkway. He did not see Olt staggering alone down to the rock, frantic with desperate rage.

Olt's purple cloak, speckled with silver serpent scales, was flying in the wind. His furred hood had been blown back to reveal his bare, mottled skull. Red and black bodies lay twisted and burned on the viewing platform behind him. The seven Gifters had paid dearly for their cowardice.

Bern alone had survived. Crouched behind the serpent throne, scorch in hand, he was peering down at the ghastly, stumbling skeleton on the walkway.

The sight was fearful. It made even the weather-beaten men and women who had stormed the fence and begun running to the rock stop short, sickened and terrified. Perhaps Hass had bullied them into agreeing with his plan, but none of them now regretted it. No one, at that moment, seeing Olt's burning eyes, his outstretched, clutching hands, could have had a doubt of what was driving him to the rock.

It had nothing to do with Dorne's safety. It had everything to do with his insatiable greed for life at any cost.

"Take them!" Olt screamed at the serpents, stabbing his finger at Sonia, Rye, and Dirk. "Take them now! I order you!"

The silver serpent shifted its chill gaze to the walkway. Olt reached the body of the stunned, curly-haired boy lying half on and half off the rock and kicked it savagely.

"Take them, you doltish beasts!" he raged. "I must live! Take the ones who are left! What are you waiting for? Do you, too, dare to defy —?"

And in one fluid movement, the silver serpent arched its body over the rock and snatched him up.

A single, chilling shriek rent the air. Blood

spattered down on the rock. Then the great serpent's body flowed back over Rye's head and into the sea like a stream of silver water. And where the tyrant had stood, there was nothing but a small scattering of silver scales.

"Now!" Hass's deep voice roared from the shore. And suddenly dozens of foul-smelling barrels were being rolled into the sea beside the rock. Buckets of grease were being flung. Bulging hide bags were flying overhead to land, splashing, in the crashing waves.

And, panicked by the sudden, overwhelming stench of what must surely be not just one attacking kobb, but many, the serpents turned tail and streaked toward the slowly dimming horizon.

The fisher folk roared in triumph. Cheering people, laughing and crying with joy, began to pour through the ruined section of fence.

"Hold!"

The order rang out over the shore, harsh and dominating. The people stopped in their tracks.

Bern stepped from behind the rapidly decaying serpent throne. "Gifters, draw your weapons!" he commanded.

The Gifters higher on the walkway grinned and trained their scorches on the crowd.

The picture of arrogance, Bern seated himself on the throne and leaned forward, the better to survey the sea of shocked faces below him.

"Olt is dead!" he shouted, his narrow eyes raking the crowd. "I am your Chieftain now!"

No one spoke. Everyone except the grinning Gifters was looking up, at Bern.

Everyone could see the snarling head of the serpent throne slowly, silently, tilting downward. Everyone understood that the head was now too heavy to be supported by the rotting, snakelike body that Olt's sorcery had preserved for so long. No one made the slightest sign or said a word.

"That is better!" jeered Bern. "And now —"

What he had been about to say, no one was ever to learn. For at that moment, the arching upper body of the preserved serpent gave way, the great silver head plunged down, and Bern fell beneath it, stone dead, two fangs buried deep in the back of his neck.

Rye, Sonia, Dirk, and Faene found refuge in Hass and Nell's home that night. Outside, the streets seethed with celebrating people, and the sky glared scarlet as the tyrant's fortress burned. Inside, all was peace.

"So we are rid not only of Olt but of his cursed Gifters as well," Hass said with satisfaction, turning from the window and pulling the curtain back in place. "There are soldiers in plenty out there, rejoicing with all the rest. But I cannot see a single Gifter uniform anywhere."

"Gifters with sense would have taken off their

uniforms," Nell said shrewdly. "But I doubt there are many left in the city now, in any case. Most ran when they saw what happened to Bern."

She winced at the memory.

"It was no more than he deserved," said Hass as he followed her upstairs to help bring down bedding for the visitors.

"It could not have happened to a nicer fellow," Sonia agreed with a fierce little grin.

Dirk glanced at her uneasily. He was not sure that he cared for Sonia very much. He preferred sweet, gentle girls, like Faene, his own dear Faene, who even now was by his side, her hand in his, her head resting on his shoulder.

Fleet had been abandoned, it seemed. Faene had told him the secret of the planned escape at last. By now, her people would be at sea, on their way to the Land of Dragons, and far beyond reach of the news that Olt was no more. It was a pity. If they had waited one more day . . .

Yet, Midsummer Eve had been their only chance to go in safety. They had taken that chance. And Faene had never intended to go with them. Faene wanted only to be with him.

Well, Dirk would take her home, to Weld, and see her settled there before going on with his search for the source of the skimmers. Faene would grieve when he left her again, but it was something he had to do, for the sake of their future. And she would be safe in the

Keep with his mother and Sonia, who for some reason she seemed to like, and Rye.

Looking over at his brother, he caught Sonia's mocking eye. It gave him a little shock, as if she had read his mind.

An odd, uncomfortable girl. Yet by all accounts she had saved Rye's life — and stayed with him on the rock, when she could have escaped. From what Dirk had seen, she and Rye seemed to trust each other completely. It was strange. And that was not all that was strange. . . .

Dirk remembered little of what had happened on the rock. He had come to himself only after Olt's death had released him from the enchantment that had bound him.

But he had seen Rye standing alone, hands upraised, holding back a sea of serpents. He knew that Rye — his little brother Rye — had saved Faene, saved him, saved them all.

The young people Dirk and his doomed band of rebels had tried to rescue from the pit were safe. Even the scorched curly-haired boy had recovered enough to smile as he was scooped up from the walkway and carried home by his rejoicing family. It was a miracle!

Hass, Faene, and Sonia had all supplied parts of the story. Rye himself, dazed with weariness, shaking with shock, weak with relief, had said very little. He had spoken to Dirk only of what had happened at home since Dirk left. The hero of the hour, he sat now wrapped in a blanket and quietly sipping soup as he stared into the glowing coals of the fire.

Now and again, he looked at the palm of his hand and rubbed it thoughtfully, as if perhaps it was itchy or sore, though it looked perfectly normal and unmarked. Then he would touch the little brown bag that hung around his neck, as if to reassure himself that it was still where it ought to be.

Dirk wondered what his young brother was thinking about. At home, in the old days, he would certainly have asked. Here and now, it was different. A strange shyness gripped him at the thought of intruding on Rye's silence.

At that moment, Rye looked up at him and smiled. And the smile was so familiar, so dearly familiar, that a lump rose in Dirk's throat, and the feeling of awkwardness vanished.

"Does your hand pain you, Rye?" he asked quietly.

Rye shook his head. "Not now," he said. "When first I was dry and the scale fell out, it did. But no longer."

"Scale?" Dirk asked blankly.

"It had done its work," said Rye, exchanging glances with Sonia. "It helped me get to you. Then it helped me hold the serpents back. I did not realize it at the time, but I have realized it since. They saw it, you see, when I held up my hand. It spoke to them, I think, like to like."

Dirk stared at him, not knowing what to say to a brother who had saved his life but was now clearly wandering in his mind.

Rye smiled and yawned. "I am not making sense to you, I know," he said. "I have so much to explain. I will tell you everything, Dirk — well, as much as I am able — on our way home tomorrow."

Dirk sighed and gave it up.

"I did not find the source of the skimmers, Rye," he said ruefully. "Olt was not the culprit. Evil as he was, he was concentrating only on keeping himself alive. No one in these parts has ever heard of skimmers. Perhaps Sholto has had better luck."

"Perhaps." Rye nodded sleepily. "We will go through the silver Door, and see."

"We?" exclaimed Dirk. "But, Rye, I thought —"

"We," Sonia put in firmly. "The three of us, or none of us."

Rye shrugged at his brother's horrified face.

"Believe me, Dirk," he said, "it is better not to argue."

And with that, for the moment, Dirk had to be content.